EDUCATION IN IMPROPRIETY

Barbara had never seen a gentleman down brandy with such abandon as Lord Damian. Especially one as otherwise appealing as this man who sat across the tavern table from her.

"Why?" she asked him. "Why do you drink so much?"

"You tell me why you're doing what you're doing, and I'll tell you why I'm doing what I'm doing," Damian answered.

Barbara could not tell him she was merely playing the part of a barmaid. She could only let Damian turn over the hand he had been stroking and lift it to his lips. There he kissed, caressingly, her palm.

"Will you come with me?" he asked. "Upstairs. Just for a little while. Do not worry. I shall take great care of you."

Barbara considered the matter. First, he clearly meant it. Second, he was too drunk to threaten any harm. Odds were, she would be the one who would have to take care of him when he passed out.

Barbara had a great deal to learn about Lord Damian Farrington—and about herself. . . .

SIGNET REGENCY ROMANCE
Coming in July 1997

Barbara Hazard
The Runaways

Sandra Heath
Summer's Secret

Elizabeth Kidd
My Lady Mischief

An Honorable Rogue

April Kihlstrom

A SIGNET BOOK

SIGNET
Published by the Penguin Group
Penguin Books USA Inc., 375 Hudson Street,
New York, New York 10014, U.S.A.
Penguin Books Ltd, 27 Wrights Lane,
London W8 5TZ, England
Penguin Books Australia Ltd,
Ringwood, Victoria, Australia
Penguin Books Canada Ltd, 10 Alcorn Avenue,
Toronto, Ontario, Canada M4V 3B2
Penguin Books (N.Z.) Ltd, 182–190 Wairau Road,
Auckland 10, New Zealand

Penguin Books Ltd, Registered Offices:
Harmondsworth, Middlesex, England

First published by Signet, an imprint of Dutton Signet,
a division of Penguin Books USA Inc.

First Printing, June, 1997
10 9 8 7 6 5 4 3 2

Printed in the United States of America

Many thanks go to Gina Haldane
for all her patience and friendship
and help while I was writing this book.

Prologue

Anyone but Barbara would have known better. But how could she? At eighteen she was lovely and lively and the toast of London. Nothing in her life had ever gone seriously wrong, and cosseted all her life, she had no notion how cruel people could be. In the end, it was that naiveté Lord Hurst counted upon. That naiveté he would use to try to destroy two lives.

On the night in question, Lady Barbara, third daughter of the Earl of Westcott, stood in a quiet corner of the ballroom at Almack's, carefully out of sight of her mother and aunt, who were happily chatting with the other chaperones, and she frowned. At once several of the gentlemen surrounding her began to speak.

"Allow me to fetch you something to eat," one pleaded.

"No, it's something to drink, Lady Barbara wants," another countered. "I'll go and fetch it at once."

"Naw, there ain't nothing worth eating or drinking here at Almack's. Dance with me, Lady Barbara. That's what you want," a third urged. "I won't step on your toes this time, I promise."

From the back of the crowd an older, wiser, more jaded voice said, "Ah, youth. How foolish. What Lady Barbara requires, obviously, is some diversion."

"Lord Hurst!" someone exclaimed, with more dismay than enthusiasm.

Barbara flushed, and then went a trifle pale. One never knew with Lord Hurst whether he meant to roast you or to be wonderfully amusing. She waited to find out which it would be tonight.

"Offered her diversion," one young gentleman had the temerity to object. "Food. Drink. Dancing. Lady Barbara don't want any of it."

Lord Hurst laughed and moved closer to Barbara. He eyed her from the top of her elegantly dressed hair to her white virginal gown to the toes of her satin slippers and sighed. "No imagination, the lot of you."

Barbara flicked open her fan and looked at Lord Hurst over the top of it. "And what sort of diversion would *you* offer me, my lord?" she asked uncertainly.

Hurst smiled and tugged one of her curls, causing a young man to gasp at his audacity and another to curl his hands into clenched fists, prepared to defend Lady Barbara should Hurst dare to offer her any further insult.

"I?" Hurst echoed. "I would not be so foolish as to offer you any diversion, Lady Barbara."

Barbara blinked and her mouth fell open in surprise. Hastily she snapped it shut, grateful that the fan hid her expression. Or so she hoped. She snapped shut *that* useful accessory and asked, with a puzzled frown, "But why not, Lord Hurst?"

Hurst smiled and studied his nails for a long moment. A very long moment that verged on insult. Then he looked at Barbara and his smile widened. He chose his words with care. If his plan was to work he must get her off her guard, engage her emotions so thoroughly that she did not have time to realize the enormity of what he meant to have her do.

"Why, I should not be so foolish, Lady Barbara, because I am wise enough to know that you would spurn any offer I might make you."

The word "offer" hung in the air as each of the individuals gathered around considered just what Hurst meant by that. When he had judged the silence had gone on long enough he ventured a further explanation.

"You are far too above yourself, Lady Barbara," Lord Hurst said with an air of false kindness. "You cannot be satisfied, save with the most outlandish nonsense and I, I am too wise to fall into such a trap. You are, to be blunt about it, far too spoiled for my tastes."

"That's not true!" Barbara protested and looked to those around her to leap to her defense.

"How dare you speak to Lady Barbara that way?" one gentleman had the foolhardiness to demand of Lord Hurst.

Hurst smiled. "Oh? You think I am wrong?"

An uneasy silence. It was Barbara who tilted up her chin and said quietly, "I am not spoiled."

He regarded her with raised eyebrows. "What, Lady Barbara? You never chafe at your limits? Never wish you could rid yourself of the rules of propriety?"

"If I sometimes chafe at all the restrictions society places on me," Barbara said hotly, "I am sure it is not to be wondered at. And you are cruel to suggest otherwise."

"You mean," Hurst asked, baiting her, "that you would rather be of another social class altogether? Perhaps you think it would be easier to be a merchant's daughter? Or a servant?"

Barbara hesitated, not knowing where Hurst was leading with his words. But he did not wait for an answer. He laughed and it was not a kind laugh.

"Oh, my dear Barbara, you are so delightfully naive!" he said. "You would never last even a day in such a role. You'd give yourself away in a moment."

But this was too much for Barbara. "I would not!"

she said. "In the country I often masqueraded as one of the servant girls to go to fairs and such."

The sudden silence that greeted these words should have alarmed Barbara. But she was too angry at Lord Hurst to notice. Or to heed the warning gleam in his eyes.

"Ah," he said softly, "but do you think you could get away with such a thing in London?"

"Why not?" Barbara asked, suppressing the uneasiness that began to tug at her mind.

Hurst smiled like a wolf ready to pounce on his prey. "If you are so certain of yourself, then how about a wager?" he asked.

"What sort of wager?" Barbara asked warily.

Hurst pretended to think. Suddenly he thrust a finger up into the air. "A barmaid. You shall masquerade as a barmaid. For one night. At a tavern I choose, here in London. I shall arrange everything. For one night you must convince everyone in the tavern that you are no more nor less than a simple barmaid."

There were gasps of outrage all around and even Barbara protested, "You must be joking!"

Hurst shrugged. "If you don't think you can do it—" he said.

"Of course I can!" Barbara retorted, her eyes all but snapping with anger. "I just don't think it would be wise."

Again Hurst shrugged. "Oh, wise. Well, then. A convenient excuse, I will allow."

Just as he expected, for Hurst knew his quarry well, Barbara lost her temper. Before anyone could stop her she said, "I'll do it."

And after that, it was merely a matter of arranging the details another day. No one, of course, really believed Barbara would go through with such a thing. If they had, someone would have taken steps to talk her out of such madness.

* * *

In another part of London, one of the heroes of the war in the Spanish Peninsula was engaged in the very serious matter of drinking himself into oblivion. He had finished one bottle of wine, was well into the second, and a third stood ready should he need it. It was the only way Damian Crosswell, fifth Viscount Farrington, could obliterate the images of death that haunted him.

Farrington was alone. The servants were far too wise to come near him when he was in one of his black moods. And none of his friends would either. And so, Farrington drank alone. As much as it took, for as long as it took, to achieve oblivion.

Chapter 1

Barbara tugged at the bodice of her dress. "Are you certain it is supposed to be cut this low?" she asked her maid with a hiss.

"Lower," the girl retorted and tugged the bodice to where *she* thought it ought to be. "I told you, I saw them other girls when I went round there like you asked me to. And they was showing everything!"

Barbara stared in the looking glass and grimaced. "Just so long as this is not Lord Hurst's notion of a jest," she said.

The maid seemed appalled at the suggestion. "Oh, no, milady. His lordship was most kind when he gave me this dress for you. Said he *knew* you would find it shocking and he would understand *completely* if you changed your mind."

Barbara stopped in the midst of tugging at her dress and turned to look at her maid. "Oh, he did, did he?" she said, a martial gleam in her eye. "How kind of him. But I won't change my mind. He won't win the wager that easily. I am going to prove to him, and to everyone else, that I'm not so proud, not so arrogant that I cannot masquerade successfully for just one night."

If Barbara's maid had any doubts on the subject, she was wise enough to keep them to herself. Instead, she helped Barbara finish dressing and fasten the plain dark cloak over the outfit.

"There," the maid said with some satisfaction when

she was done, "now no one will recognize you. No, nor think you a lady. You look the perfect barmaid, you do."

"Good," Barbara said stoutly, ruthlessly thrusting aside the shoots of doubt that were growing stronger every moment as it grew closer to the time she must leave on this mad escapade. She would not back down now.

"Check the hallway and make certain no one is out there," she told her maid. "And the servants' stairs as well. No one must see me."

"Leastwise not here," the maid muttered under her breath, careful not to let Barbara overhear.

Five minutes later, Barbara climbed into the coach that was waiting. Lord Hurst was inside. At the sight of him, Barbara gave a start. He chuckled.

"Surprised to see me, my dear? I can't imagine why since you must have known I would come to see for myself whether or not you fulfilled the terms of the wager," Hurst told her amiably.

"How many others will be there?" Barbara asked.

Hurst shrugged. "One or two. I have kept the location of the bar secret, out of concern for you, my dear."

"Thank you," Barbara said doubtfully.

Hurst laughed again and rapped with his cane on the roof. Immediately the coach set off. Hurst leaned back against the squabs.

"I did have another reason for being here," he said. "I thought it best if I told you a few things that might make tonight easier for you at The Fox and Hen."

Barbara blinked in surprise. "Why, that is very kind of you," she said. Then she added naively, "I was sure you would want me to fail."

Lord Hurst smiled and spread his hands. "I? Want you to fail? But why? The wager is nothing. An amusement for the both of us. A way to stave off boredom. Whether I win or lose, I shall enjoy myself tonight. It will be most entertaining. And the longer you succeed in upholding the masquerade, the longer I shall be entertained."

"I see," Barbara said.

And she did. It was just like Lord Hurst. So she listened as he instructed her in the proper behavior of a barmaid. After all, Barbara thought, he had a much better notion than she did, gathered from firsthand observation of such women.

Soon, too soon for Barbara, they reached the tavern called The Fox and Hen. By Hurst's direction they drove past and around the corner where fewer eyes would see her emerge from his carriage.

"An appropriate name, don't you think?" Hurst asked as he handed Barbara down a few moments later.

"I suppose you mean that I am the hen," Barbara said, looking up at Hurst, "but who do you mean for the fox? Yourself?"

Hurst shook his head but refused to answer her. Instead he said, "Tell the barkeep you are Henry's daughter. And he'll take you on without question."

Barbara nodded. She was both excited and terrified at what she was about to do. But if there was one thing Papa had taught his daughters, it was that once a wager was made, one always saw it through, to the best of one's abilities.

Inside the tavern, Barbara hesitated. It was lit with smoky candles and was noisy and smelly. Immediately a man came forward. The barkeep, she presumed.

"This ain't no place for a lady," the man said. "You'd best seek another establishment."

The words instantly set up Barbara's back. She dropped the hood of her cloak and said, in the rawest accent she could manage, "Caw, I ain'ts no lydie. I'm 'enry's daughter. 'E sent me round 'ere. Said you 'ad a plyce for me."

The barkeep looked taken aback but then his eyes

narrowed in the most calculating of manners and he all but rubbed his hands together in glee.

"Oo, you're a right one you are, lovey. The gents, they'll fall all over themselves over your looks, they will. Just you keep your mouth shut, as much as you can. Let them think what they like, but don't let them hear what a coarse one you are. Now come in back and hang up your cloak. The trade will be sharp soon and I want you ready and serving drinks by the time they come. I'm George, by the by. Any questions, you ask them of me."

Meekly Barbara followed the barkeep. It suited her perfectly to be told to keep her mouth shut. She'd managed all right so far, but keeping up such a raw accent all night would be a strain. Let her slip but once and the news of what she'd done would be all over London by morning.

It was not, Barbara soon discovered, that the job was terribly difficult. The men told you what they wanted and you got it for them, avoiding as best you could the hands that reached out to pinch your bottom or grab for your breasts. That was the difficult part.

Still, Barbara had begun to enjoy herself by the time Lord Hurst sauntered into the tavern, some half an hour later. He had two friends in tow and they sat down at a corner table. Hurst summoned Barbara with a look.

"Ale all around," he said.

"Ale?" the other two protested. "No, by God, Hurst, we agreed to come here with you, but not for ale! We want brandy. Fine French brandy and we won't settle for anything less."

Lord Hurst looked at Barbara and smiled sweetly. "Very well, bring us brandy. French brandy. And a glass for yourself, sweetheart."

At that the two men slapped one another on the shoulder and congratulated Hurst on his "damned impudence." They also seconded his command for a glass for Barbara.

Barbara nodded and retreated for the bar, where she told the barkeep in an undervoice, "George, the gen'lmun o'er there. They wants me to drink wif 'em."

George stared at Barbara. "So drink with them. What's the problem? It's more business for me. Though if I can, I will water your drinks, understood?"

Barbara nodded, her eyes far too large. They were making the barkeep nervous. The moment she realized George was looking at her strangely, Barbara lowered her eyes and added, "They wants brandy, George. *French* brandy. Where we going to find the likes o' that wif a war on?"

George just shook his head. "You are a naive one, ain't you, ducks? Of course we got French brandy. Send a man to the coast once a week I do, just to get my share. Here you go. The best French brandy in the house. And four glasses. Mind you get them to drink as much as you can now," he added sternly.

Barbara nodded and scurried to the table with Lord Hurst and his friends. Neither of the two young men looked familiar to Barbara, a fact for which she was profoundly grateful.

It was bad enough that Hurst had to see her like this, and that the others would hear what she had done. But it would have been truly odious to be ogled by young bucks she knew. Particularly as, under Lord Hurst's sardonic eyes, Barbara was obliged to drink the two glasses of brandy they poured her before she was able to escape the table.

Damian Crosswell, Viscount Farrington, struggled on with his jacket and damned the eyes of his tailor who had cut it so close.

"It is, milord, the fashion," Farrington's valet Phillips managed to protest.

"To the devil with fashion!" Damian retorted roundly. "And to the devil with this neckcloth as well. I cannot breathe."

The valet sighed and rolled his eyes upward but said no more. Instead he helped to settle the clothing a trifle more comfortably about Lord Farrington's neck and shoulders. When he was done, the valet stepped back and admired his handiwork. And it was his handiwork, for Lord Farrington would have gone outdoors in his shirtsleeves if Phillips had let him.

"Any further orders, milord?" Phillips asked.

"No. Yes. Go out and have an enjoyable evening yourself," Damian ordered. "I shall put myself to bed when I return."

Phillips permitted himself to smile at this jest. "Four of the clock, again, milord?" he asked.

"I don't know what the devil time I'll return," Farrington retorted. "And why the devil can't you just do as I tell you, anyway?"

Phillips smiled again. "Because, milord, we both know that if I allow you to undress yourself, both the neckcloth and the jacket and the shirt will end up on the floor, missing buttons and I know not what."

Damian sighed and clapped Phillips on the shoulder. "You're a good man, Phillips," he said. "Perhaps even a better man than I."

Phillips glowed under the praise and stammered, "I do my best, milord."

"Yes, that you do," Damian allowed softly. "And I am a brute to treat you as I do. My sincerest apologies, Phillips. Particularly as I know I am likely to abuse you roundly when I return, as heavily into my cups as I am likely to be."

"Must you," Phillips asked, emboldened by this unusual confidence, "indulge quite so freely, milord? You know how it will trouble you tomorrow."

Lord Farrington's face turned hard and ugly. "Yes, I must," he said shortly. "As you would if you carried with you the images of death that I carry. At least when I have drunk myself to oblivion, I do not dream of all the dying men I have seen, yes, and even held in my arms."

"I understand, milord," Phillips said, retreating a step from the fierce look in Farrington's eyes.

"Do you?" Damian asked sardonically. "Well, I wish to God that I did. I wish to God someone could explain to me why so many men have had to die."

There was, there could be, no answer to that, and after a moment Lord Farrington strode from the room, calling for his cloak and cane and hat and gloves. And with a moue of distress, Phillips watched him go.

Phillips was very fond of his employer but he did wish Lord Farrington cared more for his consequence. With a sigh, Phillips began to tidy up the room. Not that his lordship was likely to notice, as drunk as he was bound to be when he returned in the early hours of the morning.

As for Lord Farrington, had anyone told him what Phillips was thinking, he would promptly have agreed. He did not give a fig for his consequence. It was not even a consequence he had ever expected to have to deal with. After all, he had an elder brother. Two elder brothers. Who would have thought they would both manage to stick their spoons into the wall? Certainly not the fourth Viscount Farrington, who would never have agreed to allow Damian to buy his colors and take part in the war if he had thought there was any possibility Damian would be needed to carry on the line.

Well, he was Viscount Farrington now, sold out of his commission, but Damian refused to accept that he must be any different from what he had always been. Not after what he had seen in war. Death, horrible and painful death, made all the nonsense about titles and consequence seem hideously unimportant.

Not that everyone took it that way. It was precisely this difference of opinion which caused Damian to avoid the clubs and gaming hells frequented by others who had been in the Peninsula or fought Napoleon elsewhere. Instead, Damian had found his own refuge: The Fox and Hen.

It was late when Damian entered his favorite tavern. Clouds of blue smoke swirled through the room and the sound of voices was a noisy, welcoming cacophony. George had a new barmaid, Damian thought inconsequentially as he took a seat at a table well out of the way and near a wall. He also had a new customer, Lord Hurst.

Damian frowned. If there was one man Farrington would have preferred to avoid, it was Hurst. For the moment, fortunately, Hurst had not yet noticed him. Damian considered leaving but then shrugged. Let Hurst leave if he was uncomfortable. Damian had come to drink and drink he would. To oblivion, if that was possible.

The new barmaid stopped at his table. Damian barely glanced at her as he said, "Brandy. Two bottles. Now."

Barbara blinked. Her eyes stared, wide and astonished, at the gentleman. She had never seen him before and yet she was certain that he was a gentleman. A member of the *ton,* in fact. And since she counted every such person a potential conquest, it vexed Barbara that she did not know who he was. That mystery almost outweighed the mystery of what one gentleman would want with two bottles of brandy.

"'Ow many glasses?" Barbara asked, wondering if he had friends planning to join him later.

Now the gentleman lifted his eyes and looked at her. It was an insulting stare, one that ran up and down Barbara, a derisive smile pasted on the gentleman's face. Without realizing she did so, Barbara stiffened and tilted up her chin. Nor did his words help matters.

"Why, however many glasses you wish," the gentleman said in an amused drawl. "I certainly have no objection to you joining me."

Barbara felt the color rising in her cheeks. "That's not what I meant!" she said.

His eyes snapped wide open. He leaned forward, his arms on the table. His feet were suddenly planted flat on the floor. "What did you say?" he asked softly.

Barbara colored even more. In her confusion she had spoken as herself and not as a cheap barmaid. Lord Hurst would be laughing into his brandy if he had seen the interchange. She must do something to retrieve the situation, and do it swiftly. Barbara had no intention of losing her wager with Lord Hurst.

"Me? Oi said, oi'm not like that," Barbara replied with a vulgar sniff.

The gentleman leaned back in his chair. He lifted his eyebrows. "No?" he countered. "If you work for George, then you are precisely like that. He tries to saddle a girl with me every time I come in here. Aye, and have me ply her with drinks. I don't mind the company and I don't mind paying for the drinks, but that's as far as it goes," Damian said. "I take no girl home with me and I go upstairs with no one. Is that understood?"

Her eyes very wide now, Barbara nodded. She did not trust herself to speak and backed away from the table, almost bumping into someone behind her. A curse was flung at Barbara and she turned and fled to the relative safety of the bar. There she tried to question George.

"Who's the bloody swell what just come in?" Barbara asked. "'E wants two bottles of brandy."

George looked to see who Barbara meant. Then he shrugged. "Him? That's Lord Farrington. Some sort of viscount or something I think. Don't matter to me. Or to you. Except he's a good customer and I want him kept happy. Do you understand me?"

Barbara nodded, though she didn't. Farrington. Who hadn't heard of the mysterious hero of the Peninsula? Though there were those, Lord Hurst among them, who said that any man who hid from the *ton* as Farrington did, must have something to hide. And that perhaps he wasn't quite the hero everyone thought he was.

"I said," George interrupted her reverie by pushing the tray against Barbara's elbow, "take a second glass. Get him to pour you as many drinks as possible."

"But oi don't wants the brandy," Barbara protested.

"Want it or not, you'll drink it if he offers," George countered. "All my girls do. And anything else he wants, as well." George leered at her. Then he added slyly, "But you needn't drink it, if you don't want to. Clever girl like you ought to be able to pour it under the table unnoticed, don't you think?"

Barbara nodded numbly.

"Now go!" George hissed. "He's waiting. And becoming impatient by the looks of things."

Barbara took the tray, her head all in a whirl. She set the brandy and the two glasses on Farrington's table, then turned to go. Instantly his hand shot out and grasped Barbara's arm.

When Barbara stared pointedly at him, Farrington laughed and let go. His voice was taunting as he said, "What? Didn't George give you your orders? Come. Sit and have a drink with me."

Chapter 2

With a quick glance over her shoulder, Barbara saw that Lord Hurst was watching with great interest. There was a sinking sensation in her stomach and a weak smile upon her face as Barbara took the seat opposite Lord Farrington.

"That's better," he said encouragingly and poured both of them a drink. "Cheers," he added as he raised his glass and waited for Barbara to raise hers.

Still smiling weakly, Barbara did so. It was her third glass of the night and she sipped tentatively, already knowing she disliked the taste. She almost choked as the brandy burned its way down her throat again. She was horrified to see Lord Farrington toss his brandy down in one gulp and instantly reach for the bottle to refill his glass.

As Barbara watched, Farrington leaned back in his chair and regarded her with great interest. Barbara dared not meet his eyes and looked at her glass instead. It was a mistake. Just the thought of drinking more set her stomach to protesting the possibility.

"You puzzle me," Lord Farrington said, interrupting Barbara's thoughts and causing her to look at him warily.

Farrington studied Barbara, then leaned forward. Barbara leaned back. Farrington stopped, and even retreated. Barbara breathed a sigh of relief.

"I puzzles you, sir?" Barbara ventured to ask.

Farrington tossed off his second glass and poured a

third. This one he studied for several moments before he answered her. "Yes, you puzzle me," he said at last, just when Barbara had finally begun to relax. "You don't like brandy. You're ill at ease when a man stares at you. You have"—Farrington paused and drew his brows together in a frown—"an air, almost, of innocence about you that matches neither your clothes nor your surroundings."

Barbara held her breath. This was disaster! One word and Hurst would have won. Before the night was even a quarter over. It was unthinkable, unbearable, and for a moment Barbara thought she was going to cry.

Something of Barbara's distress must have conveyed itself to Lord Farrington, because his own expression softened. "Don't worry," he said gently. "I shan't cause you any trouble. I *think* I like you."

Barbara almost laughed at his uncertainty. "I thinks you're almost drunk, milord," she retorted, but without any malice.

Farrington paused in the act of raising his glass to his lips. He tilted his head to one side and then answered her. "No, I am not drunk yet. Not nearly so. But I will be. It is"—his lips quirked in a self-deprecating smile as he said—"both my habit and my need."

Barbara wanted to reach out and touch his arm. To ask Lord Farrington what wound to his soul could possibly be so grave as to drive him to drink himself to oblivion every night. And to ask if she could, in any way, help him find a way to heal.

But that was absurd. To say such a thing would not only reveal her masquerade, but bring down his ridicule upon her head. What man wanted words put to his pain? What man wanted some unknown woman to offer unlooked-for sympathy? By her own experience Barbara knew it was the surest path to drive a man away.

Again it was as though Lord Farrington could read Barbara's thoughts. He set down his glass and took hers from her unprotesting fingers.

"You don't need to do this," he said. Gently. Softly. Kindly.

Barbara blinked back unexpected tears. "Yes, Oi do," she countered.

"Why? George?" Farrington demanded.

Barbara shook her head. It wasn't right, it wasn't fair that Lord Farrington should look at her with such kindness and understanding in his eyes. In a moment she would be entirely undone. And ruined. With not even the consolation of having won the wager.

Farrington sighed. "Don't cry," he said. "I shan't complain about you to George."

Barbara took a deep breath. She had to compose herself. She tossed her head in imitation of the careless gesture the other barmaids used. "Oi'm not afraid," she said.

Farrington smiled a bittersweet smile and picked up his glass again. Suddenly he stopped smiling and stared at a point over Barbara's head. Slowly, warily, Barbara turned to see who the viscount was staring at.

Lord Hurst looked down at her through his quizzing glass, then let it drop. To the viscount he said in a taunting tone, "Your taste is abominable, Farrington."

Barbara flinched. She had never heard Hurst sound so cruel. And given his nature, that was cruel indeed. But why was he directing it at her?

He wasn't. Hurst's next words made plain that his venom was aimed at Farrington. "But then, I should have expected your tastes to be low. You avoid all the eligible ladies of the *ton* and consort, instead, with London barmaids," Hurst said derisively.

Farrington's eyes narrowed. His mouth became a thin, harsh line slashing across his face. His voice was level but with a deadly undercurrent beneath the calm.

"You are insulting the lady," Farrington answered curtly.

"*Lady?*" Hurst echoed in incredulous tones. He laughed. "Look again, Farrington, she's a barmaid. A common London barmaid! Or are you so drunk you think her a member of the *ton*?"

Lord Hurst was baiting both of them, Barbara decided, without being able to understand why. Oh, she understood well enough that Lord Hurst hoped to goad her into revealing who she was. But what Barbara could not understand was what he hoped to accomplish with Farrington.

The viscount rose lazily to his feet. Farrington towered over Lord Hurst by a good six inches. He leaned toward Hurst. "I don't give a damn about her rank," Farrington said, biting off each word precisely. "This girl does not deserve your insults."

"My, you are ardent in her defense," Hurst said mildly. "Are we to expect wedding bells? No, of course not. Even you would not so far forget what is due to your rank. Not, of course, out of any true feeling for the same, but out of regard for the feelings of your family, I suppose."

Farrington's face turned alarmingly dark. Barbara started to rise to her feet to intervene. She would reveal her name, lose the wager, risk censure, before she would allow matters to go any further.

But someone was before Barbara. A booming voice behind them all said, "Now, now, what's this, gents? Fighting? Not in The Fox and Hen you don't."

Farrington took a deep breath and sat down. "My apologies, George. I forgot myself."

Barbara sank back onto her own chair with a sigh of relief. Above her Lord Hurst regarded the proprietor for a long moment, then he smiled. His voice was warm, belying the cruelty that had been present mere moments before.

"Alas, George, is it? My apologies, as well. I cannot think how I could so far forget myself as to allow matters to come to such a pass. Enjoy the rest of your evening here, milord," Hurst told Farrington.

Then, with a flick of his finger at Barbara's cheek, Hurst sauntered back to his friends. Farrington looked at Barbara with an apology in his eyes that filled her with an unexpected sense of guilt. What would he think, she wondered, if he knew of the wager that she and Lord Hurst had concocted between them?

"Is there anything else you would like?" George was asking Farrington. "More brandy? A different girl, perhaps? I see she is not drinking with you. Does she displease you, then?"

"No!"

Farrington's answer was instant and sharp. He paused and added, more calmly, with a lazy drawl to his voice, "I like this girl, George. She is by far the best you have hired since I came to London."

George seemed to relax and he smiled broadly. He placed a hand on Barbara's shoulder, however, and squeezed it tightly in warning as he said, "I am delighted you are pleased, milord. And I assure you she is also most willing and eager to please you, in *any* way you choose, milord. Ain't you, lovey?" Then George leaned over and whispered fiercely into Barbara's ear, "Drink your brandy, girl!"

Barbara smiled weakly and picked up the glass. Under George's baleful eye she downed it as quickly as possible. Farrington frowned, but at George's suggestion poured her another. Only after he saw her drink that as well, did George leave the table.

Farrington continued to frown and Barbara dared not look directly at him. He also continued to drink as if the brandy were water, growing steadily more inebriated as Barbara watched with a sense of confusion and alarm. After only four glasses her own head spun, how must his feel after so many more?

"Why?" she asked, when she could stand it no longer. "Why do you drink so much?"

"You tell me why you're doing what you're doing, and I'll tell you why I'm doing what I'm doing," Farrington countered with a triumphant grin.

Barbara shook her head, trying to clear it. She shouldn't have come tonight. She shouldn't have accepted the wager. And most important, she shouldn't have drunk so much brandy. But it was far too late to remedy any one of those errors, and in answer she picked up her glass and drank some more. Tomorrow she would realize what an error that had been but at the time, with several glasses of brandy already in her, it seemed like a perfectly reasonable way to avoid answering Lord Farrington's questions.

But Farrington was not to be evaded so easily. He reached out and captured her hand with his own. "Why?" his voice came softly across the table. "Are you alone? Adrift in the world? Must you depend upon George's hiring you to survive? What is it that brings you to such a place?"

When Barbara still did not answer, Farrington turned over the hand he had been stroking and lifted it to his lips. There he kissed, caressingly, her palm.

He was drunk, very drunk. Drunker than he could ever remember being before. But it didn't matter. Nothing seemed to matter. Except being here with this girl.

"I have never been upstairs before," Farrington said to Barbara.

The viscount was trying to speak carefully, without slurring his words, and Barbara just stared at him. She stared at him with large, deep brown eyes. Pools of sympathy that beckoned to Farrington.

"Will you come with me?" he asked. "Upstairs?

Just for a little while? Sit with me? Talk with me? Kiss me, perhaps?"

Barbara looked around. Her vision seemed to blur but she could not see Hurst. Had he gone? Left her here, unwatched? No, there was one of his friends. She wavered. She could not go upstairs with Farrington. With a frown Barbara tried to remember why. Something about propriety. But it was so hard to think with her head spinning like this.

Suddenly George was there, at her shoulder. Helping Barbara to her feet. "Of course she'll go upstairs with you, milord. Third door to the right. You'll find everything you need, milord. And no one will trouble you, I promise. Take as long as you like." To Barbara, George hissed, "Go with him, girl, or I boot you out in the street!"

Farrington frowned. "What did you say to her?" he asked George.

The proprietor bowed obsequiously. "Why, I told her how lucky she was to find favor in your eyes, milord. That's all, isn't it, lovey?"

George nudged Barbara and she nodded. Now Farrington shook his head, trying to clear it. He offered Barbara his arm. She took it, her hand trembling sweetly.

"I shall take great care of you," Farrington told her hoarsely.

Barbara smiled mistily. He meant it, and yet he was far too drunk to know what he meant. Odds were she would be the one to have to take care of him when he passed out from drink. The thought reassured her and she went willingly. But then, Barbara was extraordinarily naive.

Chapter 3

As they climbed the stairs, Lord Farrington felt the girl's hand tremble on his arm. There was such an impression of innocence about her that he wanted to shelter her, to protect her from brutes like George or Lord Hurst. And yet he also wanted her. Wanted to hold her in his arms and have her hold him, heal him, heal the wounded, hurting gash inside his soul.

And she could. Heal him. Damian knew it with a sense of wonder that filled him equally with a sense of peace for the first time since he had left his troops and set foot in England again. Here was grace and healing and yes, even the chance, finally, for redemption. All from this girl with deep brown eyes.

It made no sense, of course. And Damian knew it. But he didn't care. He only knew that he would draw what comfort he could from her presence and give her, in return, whatever she asked of him.

The innkeeper George opened the door of the room for them, bowing deeply as he did so. Candles were already lit inside, and a bottle of wine stood on the table with two glasses beside it.

"You were confident," Farrington said ironically.

"I was hopeful," George countered.

The girl spoke not a word but watched them both with wide, open eyes. Damian drew her into the room ahead of him. Still her hand trembled. He lifted that hand to his lips and kissed the palm. Gently, slowly, lovingly.

A delicate blush rose in her cheeks. God, she was a beauty! Nor did she pull away. It was as if she were drawn to him as strongly as he was drawn to her.

Damian led her to a chair, scarcely noting as the innkeeper discreetly withdrew. They might have been all alone in the world, he and the girl, for all Damian knew or cared. He poured her a glass of wine. She took it and sipped slowly, delicately, with a hesitancy that reminded him of days long ago when his mother had drunk her wine in just such a way. Before she died. Before he went off to war.

He ought not to be upstairs, like this, with any girl. But he was. And at least up here, Damian told himself, there were no eyes to ogle her, no tongues to wag about her fate. Here, alone with her, he could pretend, she could pretend, that no one and nothing else mattered.

And even as Damian told himself he ought not to reach out to touch her, to hold her, that is precisely what he did.

It wasn't real, Barbara thought. It was a dream and she would soon wake and he would be gone. And she didn't want him to go. Surely, since it was only a dream, it was all right to want to be here with him? To come upstairs this way? To let him caress her hand and even kiss it? To drink the wine he poured for her?

The candlelight shimmered and gave the room changing patterns of light and dark. Nothing seemed real, save Lord Farrington and herself.

He drew her into his arms and then onto his lap. Barbara looked, but George had gone from the room some time before.

Lord Farrington held her gently, tenderly, as though she were a fragile flower. And kissed her. Gently, tenderly, then with growing passion. And suddenly Barbara was no longer a fragile flower to him, but something to be crushed to his breast with a fierce and burning need.

Barbara gloried in the sensations he roused in her. It was wrong, a voice at the back of her head cried out to her. Dangerous. Horribly, horribly wrong. She silenced the voice. Later she would listen, but for now she wanted this, needed this, reveled in something she had never known before. For the first time a man was truly treating her as a woman and Barbara found her soul craved it with a need she had not known could be a part of her.

This was nothing like the hurried, furtive attempts of some of the callow young men who had tried to kiss Barbara. And had then stammered profuse apologies.

No, this was honest, unshielded need, though whose was greater, Barbara could not have said. And then he set her down. Off his lap and standing on her feet. He was breathing heavily, though no more heavily than she.

"Sit," Lord Farrington said hoarsely. "Sit. Sit and let me just look at you. Otherwise I shall not be responsible for my actions."

"Why?" Barbara could not help but ask. "Why do I matter to you?"

"Because you are my salvation," he replied.

"You're drunk," Barbara accused. "Three sheets to the wind. Ready to cast up your accounts, I daresay."

"So are you," Farrington countered.

"So am I," Barbara gravely agreed.

And then Farrington poured them both more wine. As he sipped from his glass he said abruptly, "Why are you here? Is it money?"

What should she say? Barbara could not tell him the truth. And yet, was it a lie to say it was for money? After all there was a wager at the base of it all.

"Yes, for money," Barbara replied, drinking from her own glass.

Farrington tugged and patted at his pockets and in the end pulled out a sheaf of bank notes. He thrust them at her. "Take these," he said roughly. "You do not belong here. Go and never come back. If this is not enough, tell me and tomorrow I will send you more."

Barbara stared blankly at the money before her. She could not take it and yet how could she refuse? Farrington misunderstood. His voice was low and urgent as he told her, "It is not to buy you! Take it and go. This very minute, if you wish. Only take it. Take it and find a way to support yourself that does not require you to work in this tawdry, appalling inn."

That made Barbara smile unsteadily. She took a sip of wine and over the top of her glass she looked at him and said, "You came here. You cannot think it so very bad a place if you came here, can you?"

Farrington leaned toward her. The effects of all the wine and brandy were apparent in every move he made, in his eyes, and in the way he blurred his speech.

"It is not so very bad for me," he told her fiercely, "but it is very bad for you. This place will wear you down, scarcely before you know it. Destroy you, if you do not take care. Take the money. Go. It does not obligate you in any way to me."

Still Barbara did not touch the money. She scarcely noticed it. All she could think of was that he was trying to send her away. Her lips trembled, as did her voice, as she said, "You want me to go? You are tired of my company already?"

Farrington grasped his head in his hands. "No!" he all but shouted with eyes closed. Then he opened his eyes and grabbed for Barbara's hand. He held it with a fierceness that almost made her cry out in pain. "I don't want you to go," he said. "I don't want you to leave. But neither do I want you to feel I am buying you. I want to know that if you stay, it is of your own free will. And if you go, then I will wish you Godspeed."

"And you will drink yourself to the floor," Barbara said, with sudden understanding.

Slowly Farrington let go of her hand. He leaned back in his chair and there was despair in his eyes and in his voice as he replied, scarcely above a whisper, "Yes, and I will drink myself to the floor."

Barbara reached out, wanting to brush the errant lock of hair out of Lord Farrington's eyes. Wanting to stroke his cheek and murmur soothing words until the look of despair on his face disappeared.

But all Barbara said aloud was, "Then I shall stay."

Hope leapt in Farrington's eyes. "Of your own freewill?" he asked.

"Of my own free will," Barbara agreed.

Hesitantly, as though he scarcely dared believe, scarcely dared hope, Farrington reached out until his hand touched hers again.

"Will you dance with me?" he asked, rising to his feet.

It was absurd. She was a bar wench. How could she know how to dance? And yet Damian watched her, anxious for her answer.

"Dance?" Barbara echoed uncertainly. "There is no music."

But already Barbara was rising to her feet as well. She let Lord Farrington draw her to him. His hand clasped hers, his other lay gently on the curve of her waist in back. And then, to a music only they could hear, Damian and Barbara began to waltz.

Damian drew her closer. It was impossible, but she knew how to dance. She was as graceful as any girl he had ever partnered at a ball. With this girl in his arms, he could almost pretend everything was normal. That he was any young man courting any beautiful young woman. That all was right with the world.

But it wasn't. It wasn't and never would be. No matter what he did, no matter where he went, Damian would never escape the pain he carried in his soul. Unless it was with her. With this enchanting creature in his arms. She didn't even smell like a barmaid. Instead a soft scent of roses came to him as he held her close. Scandalously close, had they been at a real ball.

But they were not. They were here, in the privacy of George's upstairs room. And here he could hold her all night, if he wished, as close as he wished, and no one would say him nay.

Damian drew her closer to the bed. Again he dipped his head to capture her lips and she responded with an eagerness that almost unmanned him. Nor did she balk when his hands found the fastenings of her gown and undid them so that his hands could brush against and then capture her glorious breasts.

He groaned and bent to kiss the valley between them. She closed her eyes and leaned back her head with an instinct as old as time. And when he pressed the cradle of her hips against his rigid manhood, she did not draw away, but pressed even closer.

He wanted her and, beyond all reason, it seemed that she wanted him. Was he wrong? Was this madness? Perhaps. And yet, if so, it was a madness sweet beyond belief. Her dress slipped to the floor and his shirt soon joined it. She had more underneath than he would have supposed, but she let him remove it gladly. Nor did she turn away when he removed the last of his own clothing.

Her hands were bold and yet unbearably, sweetly shy. She knew nothing, she knew everything. And he, he felt reborn as he watched the dawning passion in her eyes. She was innocence, but innocence tempered with a joy in herself and in him and when he touched her it was as though a whole new world was opening up for both of them.

Barbara felt the same sense of wonder, the same sense of innocence and passion emanating from Lord Farrington. Part of her knew him to be a self-proclaimed rogue. Her heart told her he was a hero. His body called to hers and she reveled in the sensation of skin against skin, breast to breast, tongue, hands, all that they shared between them.

Somewhere in her mind she knew there were those who would say this was wrong. That tomorrow she would even say so herself. But here, now, there was a sense of rightness, of need, of belonging that Barbara could not withstand. Had she been given to such things, she would have said they belonged together, she and Lord Farrington. That they were each the half of the other. And she would have known how absurd those words sounded. Yet they were true, she would have sworn it in her heart and in her soul.

He was gentle, this rogue, and when he parted her legs and entered her, she was unprepared for the brief burst of pain before the joy. Later, when it was over, she would wonder what it meant, that brief burst of pain. Later, Lord Farrington would know for certain.

But now, together, they each found joy in the loving, in the completion, in the sense of something far grander than themselves. And after it was over, he drew her into his arms and together they fell asleep.

Chapter 4

Barbara came awake slowly. Her head ached abominably, her stomach was distinctly unsteady. There was a strange smell in the room and the sheets felt oddly scratchy. Just then her hand brushed against something. Against a body that was not her own.

Barbara sat bolt upright then, clutching the sheets to her breasts. Her naked breasts, she realized in horror as she stared down at the man beside her. Suddenly it came back to her. Everything. The wager. The drinking. Going upstairs with this man. And everything that followed.

Barbara blushed a fiery red even as she scrambled out of bed and reached for her clothes, scattered all over the floor. She had to get out of here! She had to get out before he woke and discovered her still in the room.

An ache between her thighs reminded Barbara of what had passed between them and she had to bite back a moan of distress. What had she done? She was ruined! Thoroughly, completely ruined!

How could she have done this? Mother was right. Strong drink was an abomination and led to all sorts of horrible things! Except, except that last night had not been horrible. It had not been horrible at all. Indeed, Barbara thought, remembering with another fiery blush, it had seemed absolutely wonderful at the time.

But not now. Now Barbara could only think how

one foolish wager had destroyed her. She would have to flee London. Persuade her parents to take her back to their estate. But first, first she must get back to her aunt's town house before anyone realized she was gone. It wasn't dawn yet and that was fortunate. But soon the servants would be stirring and then there would be no hope of evading discovery.

Fear lent speed to Barbara's feet and a promise of double the usual fare caused the hackney coachman she found to race his horses over the cobblestones. The first streaks of light were in the sky when Barbara finally pushed gently at the back door her maid had promised to keep open for her. The poor girl was there, terrified, as she helped Barbara inside.

"Oh, milady, hurry! They'll be up and about at any moment and I daren't think what will happen if they find you here. Come, up the back way. Now." The maid half tugged at Barbara's sleeve.

Barbara followed. In her room, the maid shut the door, then hastened to help Barbara off with her clothes. A night shift already lay on the bed, ready for her to don. The two worked silently until the moment the maid saw Barbara's petticoat.

"Milady!" she gasped. "You've hurt yourself! Been cut or something."

Barbara glanced down and saw the blood. Proof of her behavior. She swayed, then grasped for the back of a chair. Words sprang to her lips. Excuses. Talk of a knife. But the words died as Barbara saw understanding dawn in her maid's eyes.

"Not a word of this to anyone," Barbara hissed, reaching for her night shift and drawing it over her head. "If I am ruined, so, too, will you be."

The maid nodded, numbly, knowing it was true. "But what will you do, milady?" she stammered as she bundled up the discarded clothing.

Barbara paused in the act of fastening her night shift. She stared at her maid. "I don't know," she whispered, her eyes dark pools of dismay. "I just don't know."

Damian drew a hand over his face slowly. Where the devil was he? Not in his own bed, that was for certain. Nor yet in a tent, preparing for the next morning's battle. Abruptly memory returned and he sat up, looking around for the girl.

Every trace of her was gone, except those on the sheets. She had been a virgin. He had discovered that extraordinary fact last night, after it was too late to stop. After it was too late to keep her whole.

Damian felt a wave of guilt and despair. He tried to tell himself that perhaps the girl was merely remarkably adept at pretending to be a virgin. But in his heart he knew better. Damian did not think her capable of that kind of deceit. No, the mystery of who she was, of what she was, had merely deepened.

And she was gone. Of course, Damian thought with a sigh, he should have expected that. George, the proprietor, would have given her strict orders. He would want to be certain that Damian paid well for the chance to see her again. And for last night.

Damian frowned. He had already paid her. Given her a gift that would allow her to escape this horrible place. Would she take that chance? He hoped so and yet, if she did, how would he ever find her again?

Then he saw the pile of money, still on the table. A wave of despair washed over him. And yet also hope. She had needed the money but not taken it. Perhaps that meant she would be back.

Quickly Lord Farrington reached for his clothes. After he dressed, he stuffed the funds back into his pockets. For a fee, Damian was certain George would tell him everything he wished to know about the girl. For a very large fee, damn the fellow's eyes!

Still, Damian found he had no qualms in paying the sum George demanded, ten minutes later. When the money had been counted out into his hand, George grimaced and said, "You won't like this, m'lord, but I can't tell you more about the girl than that I hired her last night. A man came round, claiming to be her uncle or dad or some'un, wanting to get her a job here. It weren't no nevermind to me which it was or where she lived. I agreed to give her a try, that's all. But don't fret, m'lord. I'm certain she'll be back tonight. Come round then and you can ask her yourself whatever you wish."

George paused, then leaned forward and added leeringly, "Pleased you right well, did she, m'lord?"

In answer, Damian seized the man by his shirt with a look in his eyes that made George shrink back.

"No, here, m'lord!" George protested frantically. "I meant no disrespect!"

That brought Farrington back to his senses and he let the man go. "I'll be back tonight," he said grimly. "And you'd best not say anything to frighten the girl off."

"I won't, m'lord," George stammered.

Damian turned his back on the proprietor and left the inn. Outside he spurned the services of a hackney and decided to walk home. It was only shortly past dawn. There would be no one up and about to see him. And perhaps the walk would help to clear his head.

Lord Farrington could not say why the woman exercised such a powerful hold on his imagination, but she did. He could still smell her sweet, soft scent in his nostrils, still recall the touch of her skin, her hair, her very womanhood. And he wanted her. He wanted her more than any woman he had ever known. It was madness, a curse of the wine and brandy he had drunk. But at the moment, if it was madness, Damian had no desire to be cured.

The only question was, Damian thought as he mounted the steps to his town house, how would he fill the hours until he could try to see the girl again tonight?

Lady Westcott regarded her daughter with dismay. "But, Barbara," she protested, "we are to go to Almack's tonight! You cannot cry off. Not when I have promised my sister Ariana we will go. I think"—Lady Westcott leaned closer to confide—"Ariana has an admirer."

Barbara merely groaned and pressed deeper into the pillows. Lady Westcott crossed her arms over her chest and began to tap her foot at this behavior.

"Barbara, you cannot be so ungrateful to your aunt as to deny her this small pleasure," Lady Westcott insisted.

There was a rap at the door, then the Earl of Westcott came into the room. In his hearty, bluff voice he said, "What's this I hear? My Babs is sick? Preposterous! Babs is never sick."

Barbara groaned again. "I am today, Papa," she said weakly.

"Nonsense!" the earl retorted. "A bit of breakfast and you'll do fine."

At the mention of food, Barbara swallowed hard and had to force her stomach not to rebel. It was quite clear her family was not going to leave her in bed, and she made an effort, she truly did, to sit up. And promptly clapped a hand over her mouth to keep from disgracing herself. Never again would she partake of so much wine or brandy, Barbara vowed as her maid nervously placed a pillow behind her back.

Lady Westcott threw up her hands. "All right. It is quite clear you cannot go out today. I shall just have to tell Ariana we will go another time."

"I say, do you think we should call in a doctor?" Lord Westcott asked anxiously.

Before Lady Westcott could answer, the room became more crowded still as the family governess Miss Tibbles pressed into the room.

"What is this I hear about Lady Barbara?" Miss Tibbles demanded, advancing upon the bed and regarding Barbara with a stern eye.

Barbara shrank back against the pillows. The maid shrank into a corner. Lord and Lady Westcott both attempted to answer at the very same moment.

"It is nothing. A mere trifle."

"Poor gel is unwell, Miss Tibbles."

"Nonsense. I am persuaded she could feel better if she only tried."

"No, she really is ill, I tell you."

Miss Tibbles cut short the interchange. "Perhaps it would be best if I spoke with Barbara alone," she said.

The earl and his countess looked at one another nervously, then withdrew from the room. Even the maid took the opportunity to scuttle toward the doorway. Miss Tibbles watched them go, a tiny smile of satisfaction turning up the corners of her mouth. Only when they were all gone, and the door shut, did she turn back to Barbara.

"Well, well, my dear. So you are feeling unwell?" Miss Tibbles asked mildly.

Barbara plucked nervously at the bedcovers. In an unusually meek voice she said, "Yes, Miss Tibbles."

"I see. I don't suppose this would have anything to do with the fact that you slipped out of the house last night? Or that you imbibed far more wine than was good for you?" the governess asked.

Barbara stared at Miss Tibbles, her eyes wide. "How, how did you know?" she whispered.

Miss Tibbles advanced even closer to the bed, her eyes narrowing and her voice gaining strength. "Come, Barbara, did you think you were the first girl in my charge to do such a thing?" she demanded roundly. "Or that I would not be able to tell the signs of such behavior? Recollect that I am called in to be governess precisely in families where this sort of thing is likely to occur."

Barbara seized upon the first part of this speech. "I am no longer in your charge," she said with a sniff. "I left the schoolroom last year."

"Nonsense!" Miss Tibbles retorted. "Until I leave this household, every girl in it is under my charge! Now you will tell me where you have been, and what you have done, at once. Do I make myself clear?"

Now Barbara's eyes flashed defiance as she said, "No. I won't tell you."

"No?" Miss Tibbles' voice was deceptively soft and that frightened Barbara even more.

"Well, I did drink too much and I did slip out on a wager," Barbara admitted. Then she added, "But that is all you need to know."

Miss Tibbles regarded her pupil sardonically. "I very much doubt that," she said. "But for the moment I will accept it. Now, here is what you are going to do. I shall go down to the kitchens and prepare a certain decoction guaranteed to improve how you feel. You are going to drink it and then you are going to get out of bed and spend the day with your family, and tonight you are going to go to Almack's."

"I cannot," Barbara protested.

Miss Tibbles leaned forward until her face was a scant few inches from Barbara's. "Oh, but you must," she said. "I have little doubt that your behavior, whatever it was last night, would be sufficient to ruin you if word got out and about. Just in case there are any rumors, you must be seen, tonight, at Almack's, gay and light of heart. You must be there and be prepared to laugh away any such rumors or questions put to you. Do I make myself clear?"

Barbara went very pale, but she nodded. She was an intelligent girl and she could not deny the sense of Miss Tibbles' words.

Miss Tibbles straightened. "Good," she said. "I

shall go downstairs and prepare the decoction at once. A bath will also make you feel better. Meanwhile, I shall send your maid back upstairs to lay out a dress and brush your hair."

She paused in the doorway and added, softly, and even with a hint of kindness in her voice, "You are a clever girl, Barbara. Whatever happened, however deep you may think yourself in the briars, I assure you there is a way to come about."

Barbara smiled weakly. If only, she thought with a sense of despair, it were true.

Chapter 5

Damian's fingers slipped as he tried to tie his neckcloth. His valet stepped forward to help him, but stopped, warned off by a fierce glance in the mirror.

Silently Lord Farrington cursed his clumsiness. What the devil was the matter with him? He was only going to a tavern. What did it matter if he did or didn't see the wench again? There were plenty of wenches in the world, after all, weren't there?

As the last fold of the neckcloth finally fell into place, a tiny sigh escaped Lord Farrington's lips. No there weren't plenty of wenches in the world. At least not wenches like the one he had met last night. Absurd as his reason claimed such a notion to be, Damian felt he had met the one wench, the one woman, who could salvage his soul. And she had been gone when he woke this morning.

Reaching for his walking stick, Damian forced himself to speak in a languid voice as he told his valet, "You needn't wait up for me, Phillips. I suspect I shall be quite late again."

Phillips did not answer. They both knew very well he would ignore the suggestion.

Damian also knew very well that there was a speculative gleam in his valet's eyes, but he ignored it. He wasn't about to answer any questions, spoken or unspoken. How could he? He wasn't at all sure he even knew the answers.

Twenty minutes later, Lord Farrington strolled into

The Fox and Hen. He took his usual table and looked around. There was no sign of the girl from last night. To his disappointment, it was one of the regular girls who brought him a bottle of brandy without asking. She smiled and batted her eyes at him, but without enthusiasm, knowing only too well he would not take her upstairs.

Damian reached out and took her arm when she would have turned away. "Where is the new one?" he asked her.

"The one from last night?" the girl asked derisively. She tossed her head and sniffed. "Gone. Didn't even show up tonight. George is right mad, 'e is."

Damian let go of her arm. He leaned back in his chair conscious of twin emotions of elation and despair. Elation that she had done as he had told her and refused to come back here. Despair because he had no notion how he would ever find her again. It was Lord Hurst who came to his rescue.

"May I sit down?" a voice asked, breaking into Damian's preoccupation.

Farrington looked up, astonished to see Lord Hurst standing on the opposite side of the table, smiling down at him. His first impulse was to send the man away. But Hurst had seen the girl as well. It was possible, unlikely but possible, that there was something he knew.

"Please do," Damian said, waving a hand at the empty chair.

Lord Hurst took his time arranging himself in his chair. He snapped his fingers and the girl returned with a glass for him and he held it out for Lord Farrington to fill.

Curious, Damian filled the glass and waited. Lord Hurst tasted the brandy, smiled, and shrugged. "Acceptable," he said. "Better, no doubt, than what you had in the Peninsula."

"Infinitely," Damian agreed.

For a long moment there was silence, then Lord Hurst took another sip of brandy and asked, "You are perhaps looking for someone?"

Farrington shrugged.

Lord Hurst laughed softly. There was a hint of triumph in his voice as he said, "She won't come back here, you know. Not ever."

And then, because he could not help himself, because he had to know, Damian leaned forward. "Do you know where she is?" he demanded.

Lord Hurst smiled and sipped more of his brandy. Over the top of his glass he regarded Farrington much as a cat might regard a canary. "Yes," he agreed, "I know where she is. But are you truly certain you wish to know?"

"Yes."

Just one word. But Damian did not trust himself to say more. For that matter, he did not trust Hurst at all.

Hurst set down his glass. "She was a delightful wench, was she not? A pity, however, that she was not really a wench."

"What do you mean?" Damian asked warily.

Hurst looked surprised. "Why, just that. She was no wench. She was a young lady."

Damian's eyes went wide with disbelief. And a hint of horror. "You lie," he said, though his instincts told him otherwise.

Hurst shook his head and spread his hands, mockingly. "Why, no, I am telling you the truth. The wench you met here last night is a young lady. The daughter of an earl, to be precise."

Lord Farrington closed his eyes for a very long moment, remembering all that had passed between himself and the girl the night before. Then he opened his eyes and through clenched teeth Damian asked, "Who?"

"Lady Barbara Westcott, daughter of the Earl of Westcott," Lord Hurst replied.

Lord Farrington rose to his feet. If this was true, he must go to her at once. Speak to her father. Arrange to marry the girl.

As though he guessed Damian's intent, Lord Hurst looked up at him and said lazily, "I should guess you would be most likely to find her at Almack's. If you hurry, you should have time to go home and change and still arrive before the fatal hour of eleven."

Damian scarcely heard the words. He was too busy making plans in his head.

Barbara smiled at her partner and dipped a perfect curtsy. No one watching her would have guessed the terror in her heart.

Could they see? Could they guess? Were those whispers about her? Too many gentlemen here knew about the wager. No one, of course, dared ask Barbara if she had fulfilled the terms. It had been too scandalous for that.

Still, one careless word, one malicious hint in the wrong ears, and she would be ruined, even if no one guessed the extent of what had occurred. Why, oh, why had she ever agreed to the thing?

The murmur in the room rose louder and Barbara scarcely dared look to see if they were yet pointing fingers at her. But she must. Barbara lifted her head and looked outside the figures of the dance to see that all eyes were turned toward the doorway of Almack's. It lacked but ten minutes of eleven and there stood a remarkably handsome gentleman.

From the far side of the room where the dance had now placed her, Barbara could not see his features but she noted how all bowed and curtsied to him as though he were someone of great importance.

Prinny? No, for the fellow was far too fine of figure for that.

Then he lifted his head and looked about and Barbara froze. Some instinct told her, some unnamed sense warned her, that here he was. Lord Farrington. She knew it even before the whispers reached her ears.

"Wonder what the devil he's doing here," her partner said with a frown. "Farrington never goes out and about."

Barbara tried to keep her voice light even as she looked all about her for escape. "Perhaps he is looking for diversion, as we all are."

"Perhaps. Still say it's a devil of a strange event," her partner repeated.

Much to Barbara's relief, the figures of the dance separated them. She was spared the need to answer and she had time to think. She must not let Lord Farrington see her. Though as thoroughly disguised as Barbara had been, and as intoxicated as Lord Farrington had been, perhaps he would not recognize her in any event.

The music ended and Barbara curtsied to her partner, then hurriedly turned her back toward the door, for she could see that Lord Farrington had moved somewhat closer. Barbara opened her fan and used it, thus partially shielding her face.

In a breathless voice Barbara said, "It is hot in here, is it not, Mr. Ashe?"

At once a variety of voices offered to procure Lady Barbara lemonade, for her coterie of admirers had surrounded her the moment the music ended. Barbara smiled at them and gaily said she would go with them to the refreshment room.

Perhaps that was what attracted Lord Farrington's attention. For it was a very large party of gentlemen, and one lady, who moved en masse away from the dance floor.

She had to be here. Every instinct told Damian that Lord Hurst had been telling him the truth, if not the whole truth. And yet, would the girl really have the courage to leave her house today? After last night?

There was Lady Jersey. Damian turned to her eagerly.

"Damian! Lord Farrington now, I know. What brings you to our little gathering?" Lady Jersey asked, tapping him on the shoulder with her fan.

Farrington bowed. "The usual reasons," he parried. "Why does anyone come to these things?"

Lady Jersey regarded him with disbelief. "You? Planning to set up your nursery?"

Damian merely tilted his head to one side in reply.

"And you wish me to introduce you to this Season's innocents?" Lady Jersey laughed. "I think not! Their mothers would never forgive me."

He almost spoke her name, but that would be fatal. To draw such particular attention to Lord Westcott's daughter, to link her name with his in such a public way would ruin the both of them and that was precisely what he was here to avoid. Her ruin. And so Damian merely waited.

After a moment, Lady Jersey shrugged and laughed a little again. "Oh, very well. Now let me see, whom shall I choose? What poor lamb shall I sacrifice?" She tapped her chin thoughtfully, then looked at him. "What sort of girl are you looking for?" she asked.

Damian lifted an eyebrow. It might have been some time since he had been here, but he knew how to play the game. In a cool voice he replied, "Intelligent. Lively. Pretty. Most definitely pretty."

Lady Jersey pretended to look around. Damian waited. It would take time and no doubt he would have to dance with any number of insipid girls. But he would find Lord Westcott's daughter. Oh, yes, before the night was through, he would find her.

Barbara watched him from out of the corners of her eyes. He was dancing. The notorious, reclusive Lord Farrington was dancing. But not with her.

Barbara tried to tell herself it was for the best. She tried to tell herself that the best thing that could happen was that Lord Farrington should pay her no attention. That she should go unrecognized to him and that she should pray he forget the night had ever occurred.

But it was useless. Again and again Barbara found her eyes straying to where he was. Remembering. Not only her ruin but also what had come before. His gentleness. Lord Farrington's desire to help a poor bar wench, a girl he didn't even know.

"Are you all right?" her partner asked.

With a wince, Barbara realized she had just stepped on his toes for the third time tonight.

"I pray your pardon," she said, moving with the figures of the dance. "I have a touch of the headache."

"I shall take you back to your mother the moment this dance is ended," the young gentleman promised.

But fortune intervened. Scarcely had the music ceased than Lord Farrington was before her, bowing, soliciting her hand for the next dance. Barbara looked at him helplessly. The young gentleman started to protest. She gave Lord Farrington her hand anyway.

The musicians struck up and Barbara realized, with a sense of panic, that they were beginning a waltz. No, she could not do this! But already Lord Farrington's hand was on the small of her back, his other clasping hers firmly.

Barbara looked up at him. His face held no expression other than the polite one it had held for every other girl he had danced with tonight. Perhaps, she thought, he did not recognize her. Yet. But for Barbara it was a poignant reminder of the dance they had danced the night before. And all that came after it. Suddenly, in his arms, she remembered every kiss, every touch, every sensation, every intimate moment that had passed between them. How could he not remember? And yet, it seemed he did not.

"I collect you are the Earl of Westcott's daughter," Lord Farrington said coolly as he whirled her about the room.

"Yes," Barbara managed to stammer. "The third of five."

"Five sisters? A large family then," Farrington said. "Have you been in London long?"

Barbara missed a step and he caught her effortlessly. "I, no, yes, that is, this is my second Season," she said.

"I see. And do you like London?" Farrington persisted.

What should she say? What could she say? Were his words mere polite conversation? Or was there some hidden meaning behind them? Barbara had never felt more wretched in her life and she hadn't the faintest notion what to do.

"Surely," Farrington prodded her sardonically, "it is not such a difficult question."

That did it! Now he had roused her anger and Barbara's head snapped up to answer him. "I find London quite fascinating," she said. "Though I think that in many ways, I like the country far better."

"Fewer opportunities to land oneself in the briars?" Farrington asked softly.

Barbara's eyes widened. He nodded ever so slightly. "I shall be calling upon your father in the morning," Farrington added in the sternest of voices.

And what was there to say to that? Her mind all a whirl, Barbara was quite content to dance the rest of the waltz without the least conversation between herself and Lord Farrington.

Chapter 6

The Earl of Westcott stared at the gentleman on the other side of the large, polished desk. "You what?" he asked in disbelief.

Lord Farrington crossed his legs and stared coolly back. "I have come to ask permission to court your daughter Barbara. To ask, in fact, for her hand in marriage."

"But you don't even know the girl!" Westcott protested.

"That is a matter which can be remedied," Farrington parried.

"Why?" Lord Westcott asked abruptly. "Why do you wish to marry my daughter Barbara?"

Damian hesitated. "Let us say that I saw your daughter at Almack's last night, and became instantly, excessively attached to her."

"Excessively, indeed!" Westcott snorted. "Poppycock! That is not a reason. It is absurd!"

Farrington did not answer. He merely stared at Westcott and waited. After a few moments, the Earl of Westcott began to pace about the room. He was an indulgent, if a trifle distant father, but this was the outside of enough.

Finally the earl turned to Farrington and said, "No."

Damian lifted an eyebrow. "No?" he repeated incredulously.

Having made his decision, Lord Westcott came and

sat at his desk. There was no hesitation, now, in his manner as he said crisply, "That is correct. I am refusing you permission to pay your respects to my daughter Barbara. To any of my daughters. Now, or at any time in the future."

"Why?" Farrington asked. "Or rather, why not?"

The Earl of Westcott leaned back in his chair. "You dare to ask me that?" he retorted. "You, whose reputation in your salad days would make a hardened libertine wince? You, who have made a career of dissolution? And since your return from the war have lived the life of a recluse? Only to appear for one night at Almack's, and in that one night see my daughter and decide you must have her? By God, you are mad, sir! Mad or worse."

"I see."

It was Damian's turn to rise to his feet and pace about the room. What to say? How to persuade Lord Westcott without betraying all that had happened between himself and Barbara? He could not, would not destroy the love her father had for her. And yet, if he did not, how could he ever right the wrong he had done and marry her?

Barbara paced about her own room. She had not slept. There were shadows under her eyes, a frantic look in them. What was he going to tell her father? Would he really come? For the tenth or perhaps even the twentieth time, Barbara snatched her bonnet off the bed. She would run away. There was no help for it.

And as she had done so many times already, Barbara removed the bonnet again and slowly set it back on the bed. Her maid watched her, a fearful look in her own eyes.

"Oh, milady, what will you do? What will *we* do? It will mean my position, I know it will! And where shall I get another after this?"

Barbara turned to the girl. "No, you shan't suffer from this, I promise. I shall swear I did it all myself and you knew nothing of what happened. You, at least, shall not have to pay for my folly."

"Perhaps he will marry you and it will all come about," the maid said hopefully.

Barbara shook her head. "I cannot marry. Not after what I have done. Not even to him. We scarcely know one another. How do I know we would not be at each other's throats in a fortnight? Besides," she said, her voice dropping as she sank into the nearest chair, "he cannot wish to marry me. The fault was mine, after all, not his. He thought I was a mere bar wench. I—I was the one who knew far better."

Barbara's maid could only watch and wait and hope that some miracle would occur.

"You turned him down?" Lady Westcott all but shrieked in the library a short time later. "Someone offered to marry Barbara and you turned him down without even asking her?"

The Earl of Westcott regarded his wife with a fond, indulgent eye. "My dear," he protested mildly, "I have turned down any number of potential suitors for Barbara without consulting her."

"Yes, but they were all gazetted fortune hunters, or wastrels," Lady Westcott protested. "Not a gentleman with a title and ten thousand pounds a year! This is quite, quite different."

Lord Westcott sighed. "Yes, my dear," he said seriously, "it is quite different. Lord Farrington, for all his title, has a worse reputation than any of them."

"Oh, pooh, that was years ago," Lady Westcott retorted. "In his salad days. I daresay he has improved greatly. He must have. He was an officer, fighting in the Peninsula. Perhaps he has matured."

"Very well," Lord Westcott said reasonably, "suppose he has. Then tell me, why should he wish to marry Barbara when he has only seen her once? Something havey-cavey there. Even you cannot pretend otherwise, m'dear."

"Pretend? Nothing of the sort," Lady Westcott said stoutly. "I am merely trying to point out we should give the poor man the benefit of the doubt. I daresay it is a trifle unusual for a man to make up his mind so quickly, but depend upon it, the matter of marriage has no doubt been of concern to him for some time. And very properly so. Perhaps Lord Farrington researched the matter and went to Almack's knowing which girls he meant to choose among."

"Researched the matter?" Lord Westcott asked, turning a sardonic look upon his wife. "Decided in advance which girls to choose among? And did so upon one evening's acquaintance? Particularly as I collect he stood up with our Barbara for only one dance?"

Lady Westcott colored, very charmingly in her husband's opinion. "One dance, one evening, what is that to say to the matter? I daresay I knew my own mind about you in that short a time!"

Now Lord Westcott smiled. "Well, well, I suppose it took me a little longer, but still you have a point. Perhaps I was too hasty on that head." Abruptly he stopped and shook his head. "No, it will not do. There is still his reputation to consider. Barbara needs someone who will steady her, take her in hand. Not someone who will urge her to even wilder excesses."

"And how do you know that he will?" Lady Westcott demanded, advancing upon her husband now that she decided she had the advantage.

"Well, of course I don't," Lord Westcott began.

"And how do you know you are not breaking poor Barbara's heart by your high-handedness?" Lady Westcott persisted.

"Well, of course I can ask her," Lord Westcott temporized.

"Before the man has even had a chance to pay his addresses to her?" Lady Westcott scoffed. "How reasonable is that? You ought to at least give the poor man a chance to woo her."

But Lady Westcott had gone too far. Lord Westcott had the upper hand again and he knew it. He rose to his feet and regarded his wife with a knowing look upon his face.

"Come, Delwinia," he said, his good humor restored, "you cannot have it both ways. Either Barbara has already lost her heart to the man or she has not and it will not hurt her in the least never to see him again."

Lady Westcott stamped her dainty foot and pouted. "Oh, Adam, it is most unfair. Can't you at least ask about and see if the man has changed? He is truly the most advantageous suitor who has ever come up to scratch for the girl."

"In terms of title and money, perhaps," Lord Westcott conceded, "but not, I think, in terms of character. But," he added, almost unwillingly, "perhaps I was a trifle hasty. I shall consider the matter further."

"Oh, thank you, thank you, Adam," Lady Westcott said, clapping her hands together and coming over to kiss his lordship on the cheek.

Lord Westcott colored and pretended to gruffness, but in his heart of hearts he was secretly very pleased. When Lady Westcott had left the library, he spent some moments in contemplation. Before he took things any further and put himself to any trouble, he decided it would be as well to consult his daughter and see if she had any decided sentiments in the matter. With a nod to himself, Lord Westcott rang the bell.

Five minutes later, Barbara, wide-eyed and very wary, entered the room. He smiled at her in a way meant to put her at ease, but which only increased her nervousness.

"Please sit down, Babs," Lord Westcott said heartily. "There is a little matter I should like to discuss with you."

Barbara sat. "Of course, Papa," she said dutifully.

"Now, Babs, how are you enjoying London?" Westcott asked kindly, and congratulated himself on his tact.

Barbara looked down at the floor. "If the truth be told, Papa, I fear it begins to tire me."

Lord Westcott felt the first inkling of alarm. "Tires you? My Babs? The gel who can dance until dawn and still be up with the sun?" When she did not answer, the earl looked a little closer. The twinge of alarm grew louder. "You do look a bit peaked, child. Not coming down ill on me, are you? Mean to say that with all the blunt I've laid out on this Season, I'd hate to see it all wasted."

It seemed impossible, but Barbara went even paler than before. Lord Westcott half rose to his feet. "Here, here, don't fret! Didn't mean that, didn't mean that at all. Hang the expense! If you're ill we'll go home in a flash. Just, well, while we are still here, there is one matter I would like sorted out. You've not, that is to say, there's no one gentleman, oh hang it all, Babs, do you like Lord Farrington or not?"

Barbara stared at her father in astonishment. He had worked himself up into such a state that now he had to wipe his brow. Wordlessly her mouth opened and closed as she tried to make sense of both his question and his patent agitation.

The Earl of Westcott felt quite aggrieved. Here he was, trying to consult his daughter's feelings, and she couldn't even answer a simple question!

"Well?" he demanded impatiently. "I'm waiting for your answer. Do you like or, for that matter, have you taken a dislike to Lord Farrington?"

Barbara looked at her hands and then up at her father. "I do not know what to say," she replied. "Why are you asking me?"

"Because Lord Farrington had the infernal impudence to come round this morning and ask me for your hand in marriage, that's why! On the strength of one dance at Almack's! A crazy notion, of course, and I told him so," Lord Westcott said, warming to his subject. "Sent him to the rightabout, I did. But your mother has the absurd notion that you might somehow care. Might wish for the fellow to pay his addresses to you. So I called you down here to tell me. Speak up. Don't be afraid. Do you wish him to call on you?"

Of course she did not, Barbara told herself stoutly. It could only be an embarrassment. Or worse! And the notion of marrying Lord Farrington was patently absurd. She could do no such thing! It was all for the best that Papa had sent him away.

"Yes," Barbara said aloud.

Lord Westcott stared at his daughter, his mouth hanging open. "What?" he demanded.

Barbara gathered up her courage of which, she thought wryly, she generally had far too much. "Yes, Papa. I should very much like for Lord Farrington to call on me. At least for a bit. Until I could get to know him. I do not mean," she said, holding up a hand to forestall her father, "that I wish to marry Lord Farrington. It is, as you say, patently ridiculous on so short an acquaintance. But I did not take Lord Farrington in dislike and, well, perhaps I should be glad of a chance to see whether I like him even more upon closer knowledge."

Lord Westcott shook his head. "You've gone daft. The whole world has gone daft. But very well, if that is what you wish, then so be it. I shall send round a note to Lord Farrington saying that he is to be allowed access to this house."

Now Barbara smiled and then, to her father's utter

astonishment and her own, she blushed and said shyly, "Thank you, Papa."

Westcott's eyes narrowed. "Thought you wanted to leave London, Babs," he reminded her.

Barbara blushed even more. "Perhaps not quite yet, Papa," she replied.

Westcott threw up his hands. "Very well. I can see I shall get no sense out of you today. But understand something, Babs. Even if you take a partiality to the fellow, I am not at all certain I would allow you to marry him. He has a reputation I cannot like and if I see the least hint of improper behavior on his part, out he shall go, no matter how much you cry and carry on. Is that understood?" he demanded severely.

Improper behavior? Dear Lord what would her papa say if he knew what had already passed between them. Barbara looked everywhere but at her father.

"Barbara?" he asked warningly. "I am waiting for your answer."

"Yes, Papa," she meekly said.

"Very well. You may go now," Lord Westcott said with an air of good-natured grumbling. "No doubt your mother could use your help with something and in any event will wish to know what we have decided."

Barbara rose to her feet. She was smiling now and there was greater strength to her voice as she said, "Yes, Papa."

And then she was gone, out of the room and from under her father's watchful eye. Her thoughts were all awhirl. He wanted to marry her! It was impossible, of course, she reminded herself. But still, Lord Farrington had told her father he wanted to marry her!

Without understanding why, Barbara was conscious of a lightness to her heart, all out of proportion to the temperate terms in which her father had agreed to allow Lord Farrington access to the house.

Upstairs, Barbara found her mother closeted with Miss Tibbles. Barbara would have retreated but neither woman let her.

"Come in, my dear," Lady Westcott said eagerly, "and tell me what your papa decided."

Once again Barbara sat and stared at the floor with unaccustomed meekness as she answered her mother. "Lord Farrington is to be allowed to call," she said.

Lady Westcott clapped her hands together in delight. "Excellent. I knew it would all come about. Such a handsome man and with excellent address. And ten thousand pounds a year, so we need have no fear he is a fortune hunter."

Lady Westcott rattled on for some minutes and gradually Barbara began to cheer up. If her mother thought it a good notion and she did decide she could wed Lord Farrington, then all might be well after all.

Only Miss Tibbles was silent, murmuring appropriate comments when applied to by Lady Westcott but otherwise saying nothing. And as Lady Westcott grew more animated, Miss Tibbles' own expression grew more grim. Whatever the countess might think, or her wayward daughter, there was disaster in the air. Miss Tibbles felt it in her bones. And on this point, Miss Tibbles was never wrong.

Chapter 7

Lord Farrington stared at the note he held in his hand. What did it mean? Why had Westcott changed his mind and decided to allow Damian to call on his daughter, after all? Had she told her father?

Damian's blood ran cold at the thought of facing Westcott if he knew. Such a short note, it told him nothing. Well, there was only one way to find out. Damian would call on Lady Barbara this afternoon. His reception there would tell him which way the wind blew. And there was no point in putting off the matter.

One short hour later, Lord Farrington approached the steps of Lady Brisbane's town house, where the Westcotts were staying, and tugged at his neckcloth. Had it suddenly grown tighter? Well, there was no help for it, for the door was already opening to him.

Damian relinquished his hat and gloves and allowed himself to be shown into the drawing room. His first reaction was to recoil and almost turn straight about, for the room was filled to overflowing with young men. Lord Hurst was leaning over Barbara's shoulder and making her laugh.

But it was already too late to retreat. Lady Brisbane had seen him and was beckoning Lord Farrington forward. From where he stood, Lord Hurst tilted his head and smiled sardonically at Damian. A moment later he was bowing to his hostess.

"My dear Lord Farrington, how nice to see you

here," Lady Brisbane said. "May I present to you my sister Lady Westcott, and her daughter Barbara?"

Now Damian bowed to Lady Westcott and then to Barbara. Her lips tightened as he did so. Barbara stared up at him with wide, frightened eyes but somehow managed to smile anyway.

"Lord Farrington, I did not look to see you here today," Barbara said lightly.

Damian answered just as lightly, "I may have been a recluse of late, but even I have heard of the incomparable Lady Barbara. How could I keep away?"

Instantly there were murmurs of protest from the other gentlemen present.

"No, unfair, Farrington!"

"Trying to steal a march, are you, Farrington? You're too late, we've come before you!"

"Ignore him, Lady Barbara. He is a dog in a manger. It's me you want to favor with your attention!"

Barbara, for once, seemed not to know how to cope with all the raillery about her. Damian flushed but he knew his duty. Still, this was not the time to speak. Not when the girl was surrounded by others.

Damian bowed again to Barbara. "I shan't stay. I merely came to tell you what an honor it was to waltz with you last night and ask if you will go out riding in the park with me at four o'clock this afternoon."

There was a look of terror in Barbara's eyes at his words and Damian found himself wondering how precisely he had behaved with her that night at the inn. Had he done something he did not remember? Had she tried to fight him and he did not notice? Damian would swear she had been a willing partner, but then he had been so drunk how could he be sure?

Neither Barbara nor Damian noticed that the entire room fell silent waiting for her answer. She could not bring herself to speak, he could do nothing other than wait for her reply. The gentlemen held their breaths wondering if Farrington would succeed.

Lady Brisbane, however, was made of sterner stuff. In a sharp voice she said, "Answer him, Barbara! Have you lost your tongue?"

"I, yes, no, that is I am not certain," Barbara said, stumbling over her words. "Mama?"

It was a plea and Lady Westcott recognized it as such. In a cool but kindly condescending voice she said, "Barbara will be delighted to go out riding with you later this afternoon, Lord Farrington. I am certain one of her sisters, Rebecca or Penelope, will be available to go along as well."

It was a facer. However delicately delivered, in the most ladylike of ways, it was a facer and the entire collection of gentlemen knew it. There were hoots of laughter, hastily suppressed as Lady Brisbane glared at them, but it was enough to cause Barbara to tilt up her chin in defiance and Damian to color to the roots of his hair.

Lord Hurst smiled and said in a lazy drawl, "You are too newly come here to know the house rules, dear boy, but Lady Barbara, indeed all the Westcott girls, are most closely chaperoned. Not a breath of scandal allowed to touch on any one of them."

Damian felt an icy finger trickle down his back. He forced himself to smile and shrug as though he had not a care in the world. "Until four o'clock, then," Damian said lightly. He turned to Lady Westcott and her sister and bowed as he said, "I look forward to escorting both your lovely daughters. Good day."

It did not help Damian's composure in the least that as he was leaving the room he heard Lady Brisbane sigh and say, in a voice that carried much too far, "How very handsome he is, my dear."

Damian shuddered.

* * *

Barbara stared out the window of the bedroom that was hers while they stayed in Lady Brisbane's house, and though it was a warm day she shivered. On the bed lay the dress she was to wear when she went out for a drive with Lord Farrington. Already she could hear her sister Rebecca coming down the hallway to her room. It would make no sense to her that Barbara was not yet ready.

Barbara turned and allowed her maid to begin to help her change. All the while, even as Rebecca rapped at the door, Barbara's mind was working feverishly. How was she ever going to find her way out of this coil? She must speak to Lord Farrington alone and beg him to forget what had occurred. And yet how would that be possible if Rebecca were there?

But if Barbara did not speak to him he might say something that would ruin everything. Why, oh, why had she made that absurd wager? It had been Lord Hurst pushing Barbara to the point, of course, but that was no excuse. Her own wits had gone begging. And now, unless a miracle occurred, Barbara would be ruined and her family with her.

For a moment, as her maid did up the buttons of her dress, in a tiny corner of her heart Barbara considered the possibility that Lord Farrington did indeed wish to marry her. That it was not merely a matter of honor with him. It would have made all the difference, she thought with a sigh.

But it was most unlikely and Barbara had too great a sense of justice and too much common sense, however rarely she chose to exercise it, to believe that it was right to force Lord Farrington into marriage with her. What had happened had been her fault as much as his. Barbara could not allow him to be forced into a loveless marriage with her. Not when it would mean unhappiness for the both of them for the rest of their days.

"Barbara! Do you mean to go on woolgathering forever?" Rebecca demanded. "He is waiting! Lord Farrington is waiting for us, downstairs."

Barbara turned and looked at her younger sister and forced herself to smile. "I am almost ready," she said with a lightness she did not feel. "But it does not do to be overeager when a gentleman calls, Rebecca. You must remember that when it is your turn."

Rebecca gave a sigh of exasperation and all but stamped her foot. "Yes, but neither is it wise, I should think, to keep a gentleman waiting so long that he decides you are not coming down and leaves."

Barbara shook out her skirts. "Lord Farrington will not leave without us," she said.

"But how can you be certain?" Rebecca demanded. "He has never come to call before today and I heard you only danced with him once at Almack's. How do you know he is not the sort of man to refuse to keep his cattle waiting?"

Barbara shook her head but at the same time started for the door. "He will not leave without us," she repeated, "but come. I have no wish to keep him waiting any longer."

Rebecca followed, muttering dark imprecations as to her sister's behavior and how different her own would be when it was her turn to have a Season.

Lord Farrington sat, most properly, in the drawing room with Lady Brisbane and Lady Westcott. Outwardly he was all amiability, inwardly he seethed, wishing Barbara and her sister would hurry.

It was agony to be here. To be under the watchful gaze of two ladies and know that if they had any notion what had passed between himself and their cherished Barbara they would have driven him into the street with a whip.

Finally Barbara and another girl entered the room. Lady Westcott rose to her feet and Damian quite naturally followed suit.

"Lord Farrington," the countess said, "this is Rebecca, my youngest daughter. She will accompany you and Barbara on your drive in the park."

What was there to do but bow and accept the inevitable gracefully? And yet there was a bleak look in Farrington's eyes that did not escape Barbara's notice.

So he did feel trapped. Barbara wished it were not so. But she was trapped as well. No more than Lord Farrington could she decline her sister's company. No more than Lord Farrington could she ignore the conversation they must at some point have.

But Lord Farrington was speaking, murmuring the usual conventional words, and now they were moving to the front hall. Was her dress of vivid green flattering? Or did it only remind him of her bold behavior? Would he have preferred that Barbara dress in the demure colors of pale jonquil or pale rose that her sisters Rebecca and Penelope wore? These thoughts and more plagued Barbara as Lord Farrington handed her into his carriage.

Rebecca was aware of none of this. She breathed a sigh of admiration as Lord Farrington's tiger let go of the horses and sprang to his post at the back of the carriage.

"My lord, they are marvelously high spirited steppers!" Rebecca exclaimed, unable to help herself.

Damian smiled. Here was one Westcott, at least, who liked him. "I am glad you approve," he said. "And you, Lady Barbara? What is your opinion of my cattle?"

"I, why, they are very fine. Very fine indeed," Barbara stammered.

"Indeed, they are the finest I have yet seen this Season," Rebecca added naively.

Damian regarded Rebecca with some amusement. "And you have seen a great deal of cattle this Season?" he asked. "I would not have thought you were out, yet."

Rebecca blushed. "I am not, precisely," she said. "It is just that Mama is so careful that she often sends me out with Barbara when gentlemen wish to take her for a drive. She could send Penelope, of course, but Penelope is not very fond of gentlemen and has more than once put them off with her sarcastic remarks."

"Rebecca! That is quite enough!" Barbara exclaimed, mortified. "Lord Farrington is scarcely interested in hearing about our foolish nonsense."

"On the contrary," Damian replied, his voice low and thrumming with meaning, "I am interested in everything I can discover about you and your family."

Barbara colored even more, if that were possible. She looked everywhere but at Lord Farrington and realized, with relief, that they were entering the park and he must give all his attention to handling the ribbons.

Or so she thought. A moment later, Barbara realized with dismay that Lord Farrington was drawing the carriage to a halt and handing the ribbons over to his tiger.

"I thought," Damian said blandly, "that you might like a turn about the park on foot. There is such a sad crush of carriages that I should have to devote all my attention to the horses if we stay in ours. Walking, however, I shall be free to devote my attention to the two lovely ladies who are with me."

Rebecca sighed. "How nicely put," she said approvingly and allowed Lord Farrington to help her down.

Then it was Barbara's turn. His hand on hers was agony. Every touch reminded her of other, more intimate touches. How could Lord Farrington be so cool? So unmoved?

But Damian was not unmoved. Inside he trembled with memories of his own and it was all he could do not to tremble outwardly. He wished they were alone, free from prying eyes, where he could sweep Barbara into his arms and love her again. As they had loved before.

Instead, Damian bowed to the two ladies and offered each an arm. They strolled along a path that took them a little away from the carriages. And yet it, too, was crowded. There was scarcely a moment to speak with one another, what with having to stop and greet all one's acquaintances. And while Damian had few, having played the recluse since his return to London from the Peninsula, Barbara had more than he could have imagined. And even Rebecca appeared to have her share of bosom bows.

Who were these Westcott girls that everyone should know them? Who was Barbara that she should have masqueraded as a wench and let his rogue of a self bring her to ruin?

Abruptly Damian realized that Barbara was speaking to him. "Will you tell us a little about the war?" she asked, almost shyly.

"Oh, yes, please do!" Rebecca said eagerly. "We have no brothers to tell us about such things."

"No."

Just that one word, spoken so abruptly and without hope of compromise. Taken aback, Barbara stammered, "Oh. Well, if you do not wish to, then we quite understand."

It was then that Damian turned to Barbara. And for once his face was not a pleasant mask of polite indifference. "Do you?" he demanded savagely. "Do you understand or even begin to understand how horrible it was for those of us over there? How many friends each of us lost? How many lives could not be spared?"

Rebecca stared at Lord Farrington, her jaw hanging open. No one had ever spoken so bluntly or with such force before her, outside of her own family. Barbara was not, however nearly as taken aback. Instead, oblivious to their surroundings, Barbara reached out and placed a hand on Lord Farrington's arm.

"It is no wonder, then," she said softly, "that you seek oblivion in a bottle. I am sorry to have asked you to talk about such matters. I can see that it is a wound that will take a long time to heal."

Damian wanted to wrench his arm free and tell Lady Barbara that the wound would never heal. Except, except that already there were little tendrils of warmth where before there had only been a bleak, cold space. Already, at her words, her touch, there was a part of Damian that he had folded away which now reached outward toward the light.

"Forgive me," he said stiffly. "I should not have spoken so harshly. Please, let us forget this contretemps and talk of other, pleasanter things."

They did so, but neither Damian nor Barbara could forget what had passed between them. It was as if the link formed the night at the inn had become far stronger now. And Damian knew, even if Barbara did not, that it was a link which would help to forge the shackles that would bind him to her forever. For even less now than before, could he draw back from marriage to salvage her reputation.

When Damian left Barbara and Rebecca back at Lady Brisbane's town house, it was with a promise.

"I shall see you again tomorrow," Lord Farrington said.

However much Rebecca might sigh over his lordship's apparent devotion, Barbara could not help wondering if his words were a promise or a threat.

Chapter 8

When Rebecca and Barbara entered Lady Brisbane's town house, they found the place in an uproar. A very quiet, discreet uproar, but an uproar nonetheless.

The moment the two young ladies entered the foyer, Lady Westcott appeared, almost as though she had been watching for them from the window.

"Come, Barbara," she said in a breathless voice. "Your father wishes to speak with you!"

"What has happened, Mama?" Rebecca asked.

Lady Westcott frowned at her younger daughter. "Go and see your aunt," she said. "Ariana will wish to know everyone you saw at the park."

Rebecca cast a mischievous look at Barbara that said she thought her mother was speaking arrant nonsense. Nevertheless she went. Lady Westcott became impatient at the slow manner in which Barbara was moving and finally simply grasped the girl by the wrist and began to pull her upward on the stairs.

Barbara, older and wiser than Rebecca, lowered her voice to ask discreetly, "Mama, what has happened to overset you so? Is something the matter with Papa?"

"Something the matter?" Lady Westcott hissed. "Yes, there is something the matter! I daresay he will drop dead of apoplexy this very day and it will all be your fault! Yours and Lord Farrington's. How dare he come here with such an innocent look upon his face?

And how dare you not tell us he had compromised you?"

Barbara went ice cold. So it had come to this. Someone had told her father about her behavior at the inn? Who? The answer could only have been Lord Hurst. He was the only one who knew. He had never forgiven Barbara, despite his outward amiability, for the humiliation she had caused him in her first Season. That must be it. Once more her foolishness in making that wager flooded over Barbara.

But there was no time to wallow in self-pity. They were already at the door of the library, the room Lady Brisbane had set aside for Lord Westcott's exclusive use while they were here.

Barbara's father turned instantly at the sound of their voices. He stood in silence, staring at his wife and daughter until the door was safely shut behind them. In his hand he held a sheet of paper that had clearly been crushed and then carefully smoothed out again.

Miss Tibbles stood by the window, looking most distressed, and Barbara knew that her presence was not a good omen. Now she regarded Barbara with a steady gaze as though daring her to try to lie to them.

"I have never," Lord Westcott said in slow, measured tones, "received such a scurrilous missive as I now hold in my hands. Read it, Barbara, and tell me, if you can, that there is no truth to the matter."

Barbara's own hands were shaking as she took the piece of paper from her father. There was, she noted, no signature, but the words were such that she could not doubt it had been sent by Lord Hurst. All her fears were confirmed.

The paper advised the Earl of Westcott to ask his daughter Lady Barbara where she had been, two nights before. It further advised him to have her tell him about a certain wager. And finally it advised Barbara's father to ask her what part Lord Farrington had played in her arriving home just before dawn.

Barbara let fall the paper from her hand. She could not have stopped it if her life depended upon doing so. And perhaps, in a sense, it did. The color drained from Lady Westcott's face and she clasped her breast as she exclaimed, "Is it true?"

Lord Westcott was calmer. He regarded his third daughter with an unwavering gaze. "I think," he said with deadly calm, "you had better answer for us the questions on that piece of paper."

"And you had better tell the truth," Miss Tibbles added tartly.

Barbara looked at her father, a stricken look upon her face. But there was, there could be, no reprieve. No tantrums, no tears, nothing would spare her this ordeal. And yet, no matter what the circumstances, she could not bear to tell her father everything. Or her mother. Or Miss Tibbles.

Barbara sat down and clasped her hands in her lap in a pose of unaccustomed meekness that deceived none of them. She took a deep, a very deep breath, and then she began.

"I made a wager. A very foolish wager. I said that I could successfully masquerade as a barmaid for one night, here in London. Two nights ago, I did so."

A shriek of dismay escaped Lady Westcott. Even Miss Tibbles tsked her disapproval. The earl's eyes seemed about to pop out, then he pressed his lips tightly together and waited for Barbara to go on. When she did not he lifted his eyebrows and regarded her sternly.

"Surely there is more," Lord Westcott said. "You must have had help."

Barbara did not speak. Miss Tibbles gave a sigh of exasperation. "Loyalty is all very well, Barbara," she said, "but your reputation is at stake!"

"I am all too well aware of that, Miss Tibbles. Now,

when it is too late," Barbara added, looking at her governess for the first time.

"Would that you had been aware of it beforehand," Lady Westcott interjected acidly.

Lord Westcott held up a hand to forestall his wife and Miss Tibbles from further comments. He regarded his daughter for some moments then said, "We shall come back to that point later. What I wish to know, what you will tell me, is how Lord Farrington figures into this whole affair."

Barbara was tempted to deny that Lord Farrington had been part of anything. But her father stared at her with a steadiness that could not be fooled. Not to mention Miss Tibbles, who seemed unfairly prescient about far too many things. Barbara drew her courage together, for she would surely need it, as she tried to weave a tale they might believe.

"Lord Farrington is, was, a patron at the inn where I carried out my masquerade," Barbara said cautiously.

"He saw you there?" Lady Westcott exclaimed.

"Evidently, since he suddenly came to call and asked to marry Barbara," the earl retorted sardonically. "From that event alone we can infer that far more went on than ought to have, between them."

"He, we, that is, I served his table and he asked me to sit and talk with him," Barbara said, a hint of desperation to her voice. "Lord Farrington was all that was kind, I assure you."

"Oh, I have no doubt of that!" the Earl of Westcott said under his breath.

Shaken, Barbara tried to continue. "He, I, we were seen together. That must be the reason Lord Farrington believes he must marry me. That or he was smitten when we talked."

The earl's face turned a dark red. "You expect us to believe that Lord Farrington would allow himself to be bamboozled into thinking he must marry you because you *talked* with him in a public inn?"

"Yes, but perhaps Barbara is right and he was smitten with her," Lady Westcott suggested timidly.

Lord Westcott muttered something under his breath, something perhaps it was just as well the ladies couldn't hear. In exasperation he turned to Miss Tibbles and said, "This is all your fault! If we hadn't brought Barbara to London, on your advice, none of this would have happened. So tell us, Miss Tibbles, what do you advise now?"

Miss Tibbles came forward. If she was in the least intimidated by the earl, she did not show it. Instead she calmly looked at each one in turn and then said, "In my opinion it does not matter what the precise circumstances were at the inn. Lord Farrington wishes to marry Barbara. Barbara has, by her own words, admitted that her reputation has been compromised, whether by Lord Farrington or simply by the fact of her masquerade. Therefore since she must be married and there is a suitor in hand, well"—Miss Tibbles shrugged—"I advise you to marry Barbara off to Lord Farrington as quickly as may be possible."

Instantly Barbara was on her feet, protesting. "No! You cannot do that! You cannot make him marry me just because I made a mistake!"

"There are other suitors," Lady Westcott said uneasily.

The earl answered his wife first. "Yes, and they none of them, we hope, know about this escapade. What will they say, what will they do, when they find out? At least Lord Farrington knows about it and still wants to marry the girl. Now, Barbara," he said, turning to his daughter, "tell me the truth. Is there some reason you have taken Lord Farrington in dislike? Did he force himself on you or something? Shall I call him out?"

A shocked look appeared on Barbara's face. "No!

There was nothing like that," she said. "You do not understand, Papa. I like Lord Farrington and don't wish to see him forced into something he does not deserve."

Lord Westcott relaxed. He turned his hand one way then the other as he said, "Oh, that. If he did not think he ought to marry you, Farrington would not have offered. Not a man to be forced into anything, you know. And if you have not taken him in dislike, why then I think Miss Tibbles is right to say this is the best solution to the matter. Very well, I shall send for Lord Farrington and tell him I give my consent to the match. As Miss Tibbles has said, the sooner you are wed, the better."

Barbara stared at her father incredulously, all color drained from her face. "You cannot mean it," she protested. "What if he has changed his mind?"

Lord Westcott looked at his daughter as though she had lost her wits. "Changed his mind? Surely you are joking. Lord Farrington is too much the gentleman to withdraw his offer, once it has been made. No, no, it is all settled, or soon will be. Now go upstairs, Barbara, and rest. I shall be inviting Lord Farrington to come round and dine with us tonight and then accompany us to the theater. I want you to be in your best looks. The sooner the *ton* accustoms itself to seeing the pair of you together, the better. I don't want anything to appear havey-cavey about this match."

Now Barbara stared at her father as if *he* had lost *his* wits. For a brief moment she wondered if there were any words that could change his mind, but his expression gave her no hope. She knew him far too well. With a moan, Barbara fled the room.

Miss Tibbles calmly followed. She found Barbara in her room, but not alone. She was fending off the anxious concern of her sisters Penelope and Rebecca, who knew something was amiss, but none of the details.

"It's nothing, I tell you," Barbara said, sounding

close to tears. "Mama and Papa merely mean to finally choose a husband for me."

"Against your wishes?" Rebecca asked with patent concern.

"Refuse him," Penelope counseled firmly. "Just stand your ground and refuse him. Mama and Papa cannot force you to wed this man. Simply threaten to go screaming and kicking to the altar and I assure you they will back away."

"That, girls, is quite enough," Miss Tibbles said, her cool, well-bred voice breaking into their hysterics. "Penelope, Rebecca, you ought to be at your lessons. Have you finished that essay I set you to writing?"

The twins turned to their governess and answered as one. "Yes, Miss Tibbles. It is finished. All our work is finished."

Miss Tibbles regarded her two charges sardonically. "Good," she said. "Then you can go downstairs together and each spend half an hour practicing on the pianoforte. You may turn the pages of the music for one another."

The twins groaned but went, knowing that any further protest would only draw down a stiffer assignment upon their heads.

Once they were gone, Miss Tibbles gently shut the door to Barbara's room and came to stand closer to the girl. In a voice that was devoid of emotion but equally devoid of any hint of weakness or doubt, Miss Tibbles said, "You were wise to conceal from your parents the extent of what occurred between Lord Farrington and yourself. One would not wish a wounded bridegroom at the altar and I have no doubt your father, if he knew the truth, would be foolish enough to call him out, laws or no laws."

Barbara looked at Miss Tibbles with alarm. She could not speak. After a moment the governess went on. "I do not know the details, nor do I wish to know the details myself. Fortunately that is not one of my required duties as your governess," Miss Tibbles said tartly. "I do know, however, that you must and will marry Lord Farrington."

"But I don't wish to marry him!" Barbara protested.

"On the contrary," Miss Tibbles said coolly, "you wish to marry him too much and yet feel you ought not to do so. Such sentiments do you credit. I assure you, however, that you are doing the gentleman no favor to refuse to allow him to do what he believes is right."

"Oh, Miss Tibbles, we shall end by hating one another!" Barbara said and threw herself on the bed, her shoulders shaking with the tears she could no longer hold back.

Miss Tibbles sat beside Barbara and gently rubbed her shoulders. "Perhaps," she agreed, "you will. But only if you and Lord Farrington choose to do so. Your future, Barbara, is in your hands. And it is your duty, your responsibility, to use it wisely."

There was no answer, but then Miss Tibbles did not truly expect one. Instead she rose to her feet and quietly left the room. She could counsel Barbara again when the girl had had more time to think about the matter.

Chapter 9

Damian tugged at his cravat. It was becoming an unpleasant habit of his, he thought. He didn't trust sudden invitations. Particularly sudden invitations from fathers of marriageable daughters. Particularly daughters whom he had asked to marry. Not that this situation had ever occurred before, of course, but still, it was the principle of the thing.

The majordomo who admitted Damian to the Brisbane household seemed to smile at him knowingly. He showed Lord Farrington into the library, rather than the drawing room as Damian expected.

The Earl of Westcott was waiting for him and the moment they were alone together, Westcott spoke bluntly. "Well, Lord Farrington, welcome to my house, or rather my sister-in-law's household. We invited you tonight to tell you we've decided to accept your offer for Barbara. You'll have a chance to speak to her yourself, but I can tell you now that she'll agree to have you." The Earl of Westcott paused, then told Damian, "Can't say as I like it, precisely, but under the circumstances I don't see what else I can do but wish the pair of you well."

Damian nearly choked. "Under the circumstances?" he echoed warily.

Westcott looked at him sardonically. "Really, Farrington, I do admire your discretion, but there is no need to play the innocent with me. Barbara has told us all about the night she played barmaid."

Damian made a strangling sound. "All?" he croaked.

Westcott shrugged. "Well, close enough as makes no difference. At any rate, her mother and I are agreed that under the circumstances it would be as well to marry off Barbara as quickly as possible, and since you are willing, we had best give our blessing to this match. But mind, I want no gossip! It is to appear the most natural thing. Nothing havey-cavey about it. You're not to speak of that night and I want the *ton* to think you are courting my Barbara as if it had never happened. Are we agreed on that?"

"Oh, absolutely," Damian replied fervently.

"Good." The earl smiled, all affability now that matters were decided. "Let us go into the drawing room. By now the ladies must be waiting for us."

The ladies were indeed waiting. And the way Lady Westcott and Lady Brisbane greeted Farrington so effusively only compounded Damian's discomfort. He turned to Barbara with a rather hunted look in his eyes. To his dismay, she looked as unhappy as he felt.

He bowed over her hand and Barbara all but snatched it away. Her voice bordered on the rude as she said, "Welcome, Lord Farrington."

Damian regarded Barbara with dismay. Was this the woman he was now betrothed to marry? For he could not draw back. And yet where was the nymph, the compassionate angel, the gentle wench he had fallen in love with that night in the tavern? To what misery had he, had she, with their heedless behavior, sentenced them both to bear for the rest of their lives?

Barbara stared up at Lord Farrington, willing him to understand that this arrangement was none of her doing. She was mortified at what her parents had done. She knew, from the look on his lordship's face, as her father brought him into the drawing room, that her father had told him they were to marry. And that Farrington was as shocked as she.

"You are kind to join us on such short notice," Lady Westcott said, trying to lighten the tension in the room. "Are you fond of the theater, Lord Farrington?"

"Tolerably."

"Perhaps his lordship prefers more physical pursuits," Lady Brisbane suggested kindly, "as it seems so many gentlemen do."

"Hunting, that's the ticket. I'll wager his lordship likes nothing so much as a good hunt," the Earl of Westcott chimed in heartily.

Barbara looked at Farrington and realized he had something of a hunted look upon his face at that very moment. Without thinking, without even consciously knowing that she did so, Barbara reached out and placed a hand on his arm.

"Do not let them disconcert you," she said softly. "They mean well."

Damian looked down and put a hand over hers. In a voice that was just as low and just as charged with emotion he said, "Thank you for your concern. But I have faced far worse inquiries than this, I assure you."

And then he smiled. Barbara found herself getting lost in that smile. She swallowed hard. Her mother and father and aunt were all watching with patent approval and suddenly she could not bear it. She pulled her hand free, sniffed, and moved away from Farrington. Immediately her mother gave the signal that they should go in to dinner and there was the briefest of respites.

Over dinner, however, Barbara's family continued to question Lord Farrington. They wished to know far more about him than she would have had the nerve to ask. And when that travesty was finally over, it was time to go to the theater.

He helped her on with her cloak and offered her his

arm in the most impersonal manner. Then the five of them squeezed into Lord Westcott's coach, so tightly that there could be no private conversation between any two people.

For Barbara it was agony to be so close to Farrington, to have his leg touch hers. And yet it was impossible to avoid, in such close quarters. It was intolerable when they must pretend to be as strangers to one another, and yet what was the alternative?

Finally they were at the theater. As they walked down the corridor to Lady Brisbane's box, stares and whispers followed the Westcott party. The earl insisted that Barbara and Damian sit toward the front.

"Because we want the *ton* to see the pair of you together," he hissed when Barbara would have objected.

"Your father is quite right," Damian agreed. "We want the *ton* to think there is nothing strange about our marriage, when it takes place. And since we will be married soon, it must seem I am an ardent suitor."

What was there to say to that? Barbara allowed herself to be seated with the greatest attentiveness by Farrington. He held her hand a moment longer than was necessary, his gaze rested on her face in apparent adoration, and when he was seated beside her, he bent his head so that it almost touched hers.

Barbara forced herself to smile in return. To the world it must have seemed as though they were a couple in love. The contrast between illusion and reality tore at Barbara's conscience and at her heart.

But another question nagged at Damian and bending even closer he asked urgently, "What did you tell your father about us?"

"Nothing," Barbara stammered. At his sound of disbelief she hastened to add, "A note, an unsigned note, was sent to my father. It told him to ask about a masquerade and about my connection to you. I had to tell him about the wager but I swear I told him nothing more than that you were at the inn and saw me in my disguise."

"Wager?" Damian demanded sharply. "What wager? And with whom?"

Barbara clasped her hands tightly together in her lap. "A wager with Lord Hurst. That I could successfully masquerade, for one night, as a barmaid here in London. That was why you saw me there, that night. It was a foolish wager, but I had no notion what would transpire. Lord Farrington, I am so sorry! I had not meant for you to be trapped into this marriage with me."

In her agitation, Barbara had started to turn to Damian and reach out to him. Instantly he caught her hand in his and kissed it. "Careful!" he commanded sharply.

Even as he watched her compose her features into a smile again, Damian found his own face difficult to control. A wager. He had been trapped into marriage because of a wager. And there was nothing that either of them could do about it now.

Aloud a hint of bitterness tinged his voice as he said, "It is a little late for regrets."

A tiny sound escaped her and Damian regretted his anger. She was, after all, very young. He went on, more gently, almost kindly now, trying to reassure her. "You need not fear I shall be an unreasonable husband. We must marry but there is no reason we cannot each go our own way, so long as we are discreet."

The words, so kindly and reasonably spoken, were like a knife piercing her heart. Barbara didn't want a husband who was reasonable and kind. She wanted a husband who would love her to distraction! A man she could love to distraction. But it was evident that Lord Farrington saw her only as a duty and that was a thought Barbara could not bear. Somehow she had to get out of this marriage!

That possibility looked more and more remote, however, particularly after a string of visitors to their box during the intermission. One of these was Lord Hurst and at the sight of him Barbara shrank back into her seat. He was all smiles, however, like a wolf as he bowed to the occupants of Lady Brisbane's box.

"Ah, Lord Farrington, you are here tonight, I see. I thought you might be. Most taken with Lady Barbara's charms, are you? And you, my dear. Charming as always. Do I detect a partiality toward this particular suitor? Perhaps we should lay a wager on the outcome of his courtship?"

But this was too much for Lord Westcott. "You forget yourself, m'lord," he said sharply. "My daughter does not wager."

"No?" Lord Hurst raised a delicately arched eyebrow in disbelief. "I seem to recall a wager about the outcome of my courtship of a young lady a year ago."

Barbara shivered. Was this the cause of her downfall? A wager she had all but forgotten making with a friend? A wager that she had won when Lord Hurst lost the lady to a rival suitor. Had it rankled so much, then? Had the wager with her, and the note sent round to her father, been his means of exacting revenge for the humiliation Hurst had felt a year before?

Without understanding why, Damian knew Barbara was growing more and more upset. He did not think about propriety as he put an arm around her shoulders and drew her close to him, he thought only about giving her support. But his actions did not go unnoticed. Lord Hurst clenched the back of a chair so tightly his hands went white and Lady Westcott beamed approvingly at Damian. What would have been improper in a casual suitor might be quite acceptable from Barbara's betrothed. Even Lady Brisbane gave a tiny sigh of pleasure at the sight.

Damian would have released Barbara then, but he

could still feel her shiver beneath her thin muslin gown. He would not let Hurst frighten her. Anger drove him as he said in a dangerously quiet voice, "Do you not think it would be best to return to your box before the play begins again? We shall quite understand if you do."

He felt the relief in Barbara's body. She seemed to lean a little closer to him, the tension easing. Damian squeezed her shoulder gently in reassurance and wished he could do more. He held himself tense, ready to act should Hurst dare to try to insult them again. But Hurst only pressed his lips together and bowed.

"Until another day, then," he said and was gone.

Behind him the Westcotts and Lady Brisbane murmured among themselves over Lord Hurst's bizarre behavior. Damian let go of Barbara and she hastily leaned away from him, conscious of too many interested eyes. She looked everywhere but at Lord Farrington.

"You need never fear him again," Damian said in a voice that carried to her ears only.

Barbara gave him a quick look then. "But what if he speaks of the wager?"

Damian's lips pressed into a cold, thin line. "I doubt he would be so foolish as to do so openly. It would, after all, look very bad of him, as well. And even if he does, we shall soon be married and the *ton* will look to its next scandal to gossip over. If I do not cavil at it, what right will they have to do so?"

The play had begun, but neither Barbara nor Damian paid it the least attention. She colored but made herself ask, "What if he speaks of, of our going upstairs?"

Damian's hands clenched together, almost of their own accord. "Then I shall have to call him out and kill him," he said in a cold, distant voice. Barbara flinched and he added, "But don't worry, Hurst is too much the coward to ever go so far as to give me provocation I cannot ignore."

Barbara shrank into her seat, silent, and turned to face the play. She neither saw nor heard any of it, but it was better than talking to Lord Farrington. His words and the calm way he had spoken them terrified her. What sort of man had she agreed to marry? He had been deadly serious when he spoke of killing Lord Hurst. What if he were ever to turn such anger on her?

Barbara wanted to go home. Now. This very instant. She wanted to stand up and declare her betrothal at an end before it had even officially begun or the notices sent to the papers. But she could not. Neither her parents nor Lord Farrington would allow it. Her parents because they feared a scandal, and Farrington because surely he would not allow so public a humiliation of himself.

No, Barbara would have to endure the rest of the evening in silence if that were possible. Then tomorrow, well, tomorrow, she would have to try to discover if there was any way out of this horrible coil.

As for Damian, he knew that somehow he had failed to reassure his future bride tonight, but he could not understand why. The only thought which made any sense to him was that perhaps she had a *tendre* for someone else. And that thought filled him with both cold rage and a deep sense of despair. He would, he must, marry Lady Barbara, but he wanted a willing wife, not one who came to him with tears in her eyes and fear in her heart. Yet what other way would any woman, he thought bitterly, come to be a bride to the rogue known to the world as Lord Farrington?

Chapter 10

There was no way out of the coil. Every day brought the wedding closer. It was a week before the betrothal was announced, two more before the actual event, but somehow the time seemed much shorter.

Damian tried to be all that was kind and proper but still the days passed quickly, far too quickly for Barbara's peace of mind. And then suddenly she was being dressed for her wedding. By her side were her older sisters Diana and Annabelle, their babies safely in the care of the nurses they had brought with them to London.

"You look beautiful," Annabelle said with a sigh of pleasure.

Barbara grimaced and kicked at her skirts. "I don't want to look beautiful," she said angrily. Then her face softened as she studied her reflection in the mirror. "At least, I do, but not because I am getting married," she amended.

"From what Mama has told us or, rather, from what she has *not* told us," Diana countered dryly, "I collect that you do not have a great deal of choice in the matter."

Barbara flushed. Stiffly she said, "You are not one to talk. I recall a few improper actions on your part, before *you* were married."

"Look, there is no point to this bickering," Annabelle said unhappily. "You are getting married, Barbara, and we should all be happy for you."

"Why? I am not," Barbara retorted with a pout, even as a small part of her called herself a liar.

Diana and Annabelle exchanged glances. "Perhaps," Annabelle said carefully, "I should go and see if Mama needs me."

Then, as Diana and Barbara watched, she quickly left the room. Annabelle did not, however, go in search of her mother. Instead she went directly to where she knew she would find Miss Tibbles.

Scarcely five minutes later, the governess bustled into the room, her voice beginning to scold before the door had even closed behind her.

"Now what is this I hear about missish fears?" Miss Tibbles demanded.

Even as the governess advanced toward Barbara, Diana fled the room after mumbling something about needing to see to her own dress. When they were alone, the severe expression on Miss Tibbles' face softened and she drew Barbara to sit on the bed beside her.

"It is natural," she said, "for you to have some trepidation, my dear. All women do on their wedding day. And you, more than most, have been accustomed to run wild and do as you wish."

She paused and sighed. "I had hoped a Season or two would curb that side of you, but it evidently has not and the result is this marriage. It is not what I wished for you. I had hoped you would find someone to whom you could give your heart as well as your hand. Had you been able to do so, I was persuaded you would also find happiness in marriage and not find it so difficult to submit your will to your husband's. I know that you are not indifferent to Lord Farrington, and it may yet be possible that despite the circumstances of this marriage, all will be well."

Barbara looked at Miss Tibbles. "It matters very little whether I am indifferent or not to Lord Farrington," she snapped, "for he has made it very clear that he is indifferent to me. He has spoken, more than once, of how *reasonable* he will be once we are married. How much *freedom* he will give me, as long as I am discreet. Oh, Miss Tibbles, Lord Farrington does not care a fig for me!"

The governess patted Barbara's hand. "I am very sorry to hear he has told you such nonsense," Miss Tibbles said tartly. "But life has never been fair and I doubt it is about to make an exception just for you. Now where is your Westcott courage? Your backbone? Are you going to tell me that the wildest child I have ever had the misfortune to be governess to has suddenly lost her spine? Her imagination? Her ability to turn any situation to her advantage?"

In spite of herself, Barbara began to laugh. "You are outrageous, Miss Tibbles," she said.

The governess drew herself up to her full diminutive height, and said, "I? Outrageous? Never!" Then allowing herself a tiny, bittersweet smile, she added, "I, above others, know that it is possible to face disappointment and still triumph. Do not speak to me of unhappiness. How long would you have lasted if your father had lost every penny and you had to become a governess? You will do what you must and I wish to hear no more about it. Your mother and father and sisters have enough to worry them today without your Friday face making matters worse."

Miss Tibbles rose to her feet, shook out her skirts, then looked at Barbara. In a very soft voice she added, "It will all come about, I promise."

And then Miss Tibbles was gone. But before Barbara had a chance to do more than wipe away the tears and check her appearance in the mirror, the bedroom door opened again and Rebecca slipped inside.

"You don't mind, do you?" Rebecca asked, closing the door behind her.

Barbara held out her hand to her younger sister.

"No, of course not," she smiled. "Indeed, I should be glad of the company."

"I thought you might be," Rebecca confessed, evading the hand and sitting on the edge of Barbara's bed. "Indeed, that is what I wished to ask you."

"If I were lonely?" Barbara asked, perplexed.

Rebecca ignored the question. She studied her hands as they clenched and unclenched in the folds of her skirt. "You are the only one I can ask," she said. "Diana and Annabelle have been married so long, more than a year for Diana and months for Annabelle, that they cannot recall how they felt before. But you, you have known Lord Farrington such a short time that it must still seem strange to you. And Mama, well, Mama is Mama and I can scarcely ask her. Or Miss Tibbles. And Penny, well, Penny doesn't wish to have anything to do with men. But I thought perhaps you could tell me—"

Barbara came and sat on the bed, too, and this time successfully took one of her younger sister's hands in hers. "Tell you what?" she asked gently.

Rebecca pulled her hand free, rose from the bed, and crossed the room to stare out the window. But she was too restless to stay that way. She turned to Barbara again and there was a hint of desperation in her eyes as she said, "What is it like? To be in love? To want to marry a man you scarcely know? Are you afraid? Excited? Oh, Barbara, what do you feel?"

A thousand answers came to mind and Barbara discarded every one of them. She could not lie to Rebecca and pretend it was all wonderful and yet neither could she bear to frighten the girl more than she already was.

Gently, more gently than anyone who knew Barbara could have expected her to answer, she said, "I am nervous, yes, Becca. But it will not necessarily be so for you. You may know the gentleman better than I know Lord Farrington and be more sure in your heart of your desire to marry him."

Rebecca blinked at her sister. "They have forced you into this!" she exclaimed. "Just as Penny said they did. But, Barbara, how could you agree? And what if they force me to marry against my wishes, too?"

Barbara put an arm around her sister's shoulders. "No, Becca," she said gently, "they did not force me to do this. I forced myself. But you need not do so. It was, it is," she added, swallowing hard to make herself say the words, "my choice to marry Lord Farrington."

"Then why are you so nervous?" Rebecca asked suspiciously.

"It is natural to be nervous. At least a little," Barbara acknowledged, unable to meet her sister's eyes. "But there is such a thing as good nervousness," she added stoutly, "and this is one of those times."

Rebecca hesitated, then threw her arms around Barbara to give her a quick hug. "Oh, Babs, I wish you every happiness!" she said.

And then she fled the room.

Barbara found herself thinking she wished she could flee her own fate just as easily. But she could not. Still, talking with Rebecca had steadied her own nerves just a trifle and she was ready when her parents came to take her to the church.

Later Barbara would say that she scarcely remembered anything of the ceremony. Lord Farrington stood beside her, strange and distant. She knew that the both of them answered in clear tones. But it all seemed unreal to her. Even when she signed her name. Even when everyone crowded around to wish the couple happiness.

At the wedding breakfast, it seemed that everyone was determined to tease the couple. Beside her, Barbara could feel Farrington grow more and more tense.

At one point she heard him mutter under his breath, "This is insufferable."

Barbara could only agree. And yet it was worse, far worse, when she found herself being handed into his coach, the door closing behind her, and the two of them all alone together.

Farrington did not look at her. And then he was looking at her all too intensely, his brows drawn together in a frown. It was absurd, but suddenly Barbara felt the need to apologize. For everything.

"I'm sorry," she said.

For a moment Farrington did not answer, then he shrugged. "A wedding is always for the family," he said, in cool tones. "Your parents were pleased and my relatives approve any event which allows them to eat at someone else's expense. That is sufficient."

Barbara bit her lower lip and turned to look out the window. She would not, she vowed, allow herself to cry over his setdown.

As though he sensed her thoughts, Damian leaned forward and took Barbara's hand in his own. "I'm sorry," he said softly.

Startled, she turned to look at him. He sat on the edge of the seat, bending toward her, and there was a look of earnestness upon his face. "I'm sorry," he said again. "Just because I am blue-deviled is no reason for me to be short with you. I daresay it has been no more pleasant for you than for me this morning."

"No, no it has not," Barbara agreed in a faint voice.

Now Farrington smiled. "It will soon be better," he promised. "You will like my town house, I think, and my staff has orders to see to your every comfort. If there is anything you wish, you need only tell me and I shall arrange it." He paused, seemed to gather his courage, and went on, "This has been forced on the pair of us, but that does not mean we must be unhappy. I shall certainly do my best to see that you are not."

And just why such kindness should make Barbara

wish to cry she could not say, but it did. She blinked away the gathering tears and said in a voice that only quavered slightly, "You are very kind to me, Lord Farrington."

Abruptly he let go of her hand and sat back on his seat. His voice was cool again as he said, "You had best learn to call me Damian. Otherwise we shall give rise to just that sort of speculation our marriage was designed to prevent. Recollect that we have justified the shortness of our courtship by claiming a sudden, violent affection for one another. We must endeavor, at least in public, to give some truth to that tale, my dear."

It was growing worse and worse and Barbara thought she could scarcely bear it. But she must say something! "Of course, Damian," she agreed, the name sounding uncertain on her tongue.

He grimaced. "It will become easier, and sound better, upon practice, I daresay, Barbara," he said, her own name suddenly sounding strange coming from him, though he had used it before.

And then the pair sank into silence. A most uncomfortable silence. Both breathed a sigh of relief as the carriage pulled to a halt before Farrington's town house. Now all she had to do, Barbara thought, drawing in her breath, was face all his servants.

Even that had been arranged to make matters as easy as possible. It was plain that Damian had taken pains to cause his staff to believe this marriage was a love match and not something forced upon him. Barbara found herself oddly grateful for that kindness. Every servant showed her the greatest deference and there was not a trace of insolence in any of them. They looked upon her with the same warm affection they appeared to bestow upon her husband.

As for Damian, he watched his wife greet the staff with mixed feelings of his own. She said all that was proper and acted as one born to the part. Which she had been. And yet Damian found himself longing for a glimpse of that strange creature, that lowborn wench he had met in a tavern. Was he never to see her again? Never to know the same sense of coming home that he had felt in her arms that night?

Hastily Damian thrust away the thought. The last thing he needed now was to frighten away his bride by treating her with the rough urgency he had shown at the tavern. Clearly she had been overcome by the strong spirits the innkeeper had insisted she imbibe. Clearly his own judgment had been equally impaired. But it would not happen again. He would not act the rogue with his own wife.

Thus it was that between them Damian and Barbara managed to say not two honest words to one another for the rest of the afternoon or evening. Tomorrow they would journey into the countryside for a quiet honeymoon, away from prying eyes so that they need not pretend, for at least a little while. But this was today.

And the entire household staff watched the master and his new mistress. Thus when Damian's majordomo suggested that no doubt his lordship and her ladyship would wish to retire early, he could not disagree. And when Barbara's maid laid out a night rail of such fine linen as to be almost transparent, she could not disagree with that, either.

Soon, too soon, Damian and Barbara faced one another across the width of a high-poster bed. A nerve seemed to twitch in his tightly clenched jaw and it was with difficulty that he said, "I collect you will wish your own room and one will be prepared for you while we are away.. But for tonight it would be best if we shared this one and gave the servants no cause for gossip."

Barbara felt her breath catch in her throat and it was only with an effort that she managed to reply, "Yes, of course, obviously you are right."

Still they stared at one another. Barbara shivered under the force of his gaze, something dark and fiery-hooded in Damian's eyes.

"Perhaps you had best get into bed," he said, mistaking the cause of her tremor. "It will be warmer under the covers."

Barbara hesitated. "I am not cold," she answered.

He came around the bed and she backed away. "Frightened?" Damian demanded and his eyes narrowed to little more than slits.

Barbara tilted up her chin. "A Westcott is not frightened of anything," she replied.

Damian smiled. Damn the man, he smiled. Did he have to smile? And in such a tender, understanding way? And did he have to close the gap between them and reach out and draw her close to him, tucking her head under his chin as he said, so softly, "No one would think the worse if you were. This must be as hard for you as it is for me. We, neither of us, have any experience in marriage, but I must hope we shall have the wisdom to learn."

Barbara clung to him then, this strange new husband of hers. For in his arms there was comfort and safety and something much more. A warmth, a need, indeed a kind of certainty began to curl through her and she found herself reaching round this man to hold him tight. And when he lifted up her chin to kiss her, Barbara did not draw back but met him, kiss for kiss.

As for Damian, he felt himself drowning in her sweetness. This was what he had felt that night in the tavern. This was what had drawn him then and drew him still. Here, in her arms, he felt safe and warm and as though there was a way out of the trap of nightmares that had so long surrounded him.

Neither one noticed when they changed floor for bed or lost the clothing that hampered access between them. But sometime later, much later, they fell asleep in one another's arms, both optimistic for the future.

Chapter 11

Lady Westcott looked at her husband affectionately. "You do think it will be all right between them, Barbara and Lord Farrington, I mean, don't you, Adam?" she asked.

The Earl of Westcott knew better than to attempt to hold his wife close, even after marital affections had been exchanged. He lay the precise distance away from her that he knew to be her preference.

He also knew better than to speak his mind bluntly on certain matters. It was late enough as it was and he had no desire to be kept awake the rest of the night by starting an argument now.

So, with the tact he had learned over the years of his marriage, the Earl of Westcott said, "Oh, I'm certain they will muddle through, m'dear. And if they are lucky they shall be as happy as we have been."

It was a stroke of genius to say so. Lady Westcott sighed and actually leaned forward to kiss her husband on the cheek before she hastily retreated to her side of the bed again. And then they both settled down to sleep.

"No! Damn you, no!"

The shrieks pierced the darkness and Barbara sat up like a shot. For a moment she could not recollect where she was or why. And then she remembered. Lying beside her was her new husband Damian, and she blushed at the memory of their wedding night.

Another moan and Barbara realized that the sounds were coming from her husband. She reached out to put a hand on his shoulder but he shook it off and seemed to grow more distressed.

Suddenly his voice dropped and the words were clear as he said, "Stop. Stop right there or by God I swear I'll kill you."

Barbara pulled her hand away from Damian as though burned. She shrank back against the pillows. She didn't think he was dangerous, not really, but it never hurt to be careful, did it? Particularly with someone waking from a nightmare.

A moment later his eyes fluttered open. Damian looked at her, his face pale and savage in the darkness lit only by moonlight. He seemed an utter stranger.

Damian blinked. The room seemed for a moment to sway around him. His first impression was of a woman shrinking away from him. Barbara!

"What did I say?" he demanded harshly.

Barbara could not tell him the truth. "Nothing," she stammered, shaking her head.

Damian did not believe her. She was too pale, too shaken. He lay back against the pillows and silently cursed. So marriage had not been his salvation after all. The nightmares were still present.

He would have closed his eyes except that then he might have dreamt again. He would certainly have seen the stark images still vivid in his mind.

Barbara sat beside him, afraid to ask, to disturb him. Damian could feel her distress as surely as if she spoke aloud. He wanted to clench his fists and beat the pillow in frustration, but that would only have frightened her more. He drew in a deep breath and slowly let it out. It was over. Only a dream.

Slowly Damian sat up and reached for Barbara. She flinched. She didn't mean to, but she did. Damian let his arms fall to his side. Had it been day he would have reacted differently. He would have understood and known that she just needed time.

But Damian was still caught up in the emotions of his nightmare, still haunted by all the years of rejection from his family, even before he went off to war. He had failed them, as he had failed the men under his command. Or they had never given him a fair chance. Which one was the truth didn't matter.

Did she disdain him? Then he would disdain her even more. Did she think him a monster? Then let him give her a reason to believe it even more.

Damian didn't want to hurt Barbara, but he could not help himself as he said harshly, "Now you know just what sort of man you have trapped into marriage."

"I? Trapped you into marriage?" Barbara gasped with the injustice of his charge. "I tried to refuse. You were the one who insisted we must be married!"

Her words twisted like a knife in Damian's soul and despair swept through him. Why was he doing this? But he could not stop. He was caught up in a kind of madness that would not let him go.

Damian allowed his lips to twist into a sneer. "After you left me no choice with your masquerade," he taunted Barbara. "You made an extraordinarily convincing wench, dear wife. Unfortunately for me I had, however belatedly, some sense of honor."

She rose from the bed, needing to put a distance between herself and Damian. Clearly some private demons drove him to say these things, things he could not possibly mean. When she was safely far away, she turned on him.

"Why?" Barbara demanded. "Why are you trying to do this, Damian? Why are you trying to drive me away? You know as well as I do that I was reluctant to marry you. That I did not mean to hold you to your sense of honor. As of yesterday you understood that perfectly well. So why, now, Damian, do you charge me with things you do not, cannot, believe?"

He looked away. Every word she spoke was the truth, but he could not allow her to see that he knew that, or to acknowledge it, even in his own heart. He could not allow Barbara to hurt him. Not the way he had been hurt before. Easier, far easier, to drive her away before she could reject him. So he chose the most cutting words he could find, the most sardonic tone of voice.

"What a touching declaration of innocence, my dear. But then I already knew you to be a superb actress," Damian said sardonically. "What part will you enact me next? Any but the devoted wife, I suppose. That would be hard after you have so recently shrunk away when I reached for you."

Barbara gasped in outrage, then her eyes narrowed. "You would have shrunk away from yourself as well," she said tartly, "if you could have heard yourself right before you woke. Anyone sane would have done so."

So he had spoken in his sleep! Damian threw aside the covers and got to his feet. He padded toward her. "What did I say?" he demanded, fear twisting his features, lending harshness to his voice.

Barbara backed away from him. Every moment Damian seemed more a stranger, frighteningly so. Her own voice was scarcely above a whisper as she replied, "You said, 'Stop or I'll kill you!' "

But it was Damian who stopped. Stopped and had to fight the urge to bury his face in his hands. That would help nothing. Instead he just stood there. Staring at nothing. Remembering.

"Who—who were you going to kill?" Barbara asked, unable to help herself.

Damian's head snapped up and he stared at her, his eyes seeming to glow in the darkness. "It was war," he said, biting off the words. "There were many men, too many men, I had to kill."

She should have been frightened, and she was, but Barbara had been born to fight for what she wanted, fight for those she cared about. And, despite everything, she cared about Damian. Something, some instinct, made her ask softly, "Yes, but who, among all those men, is it that haunts your dreams?"

It was the kindness, the gentleness that was Damian's undoing. He thought he had long ago forfeited such things, if indeed he had ever known them. He could not bear the emotions her kindness roused in him and he turned away.

Over his shoulder Damian said harshly, "You know nothing of it!"

He heard her footsteps, soft in the night, and had to force himself not to run from them. Then her hand touched his shoulder gently, and she said, "Of course I know nothing. That is why I asked."

He could not fight her any longer, Damian thought. With a groan he turned and drew Barbara into his arms and buried his face in her hair. If she turned away from him in the morning, so be it. Here, now, for a moment, there would be comfort and the faintest hint of peace.

Barbara did not press Damian any longer for an answer. There would be time enough for that tomorrow. When the nightmares were burned away by the light of day. When he could look at her and not simply see the demons that chased him in the darkness.

Together they made their way back to the bed and to loving. A fiercer, more urgent loving than before. And yet, even in the fierceness there was gentleness, a need not to hurt one another.

When he had spent himself, Damian fell asleep beside his bride. Tomorrow, tomorrow they would have to sort things out, he told himself, but tonight he would sleep.

Barbara, however, lay awake for a long time beside her new husband. Already she thought she loved him. And yet there was a part of her that was frightened of him. Of what he had cried out in his sleep. She knew Damian had been a soldier and she was not so foolish as to believe one could win a war without causing death. But there was something more to it here than that, Barbara was certain.

Who had he threatened to kill? She could not help but wonder. And had he done so? Her instincts told her that Damian was a good and honorable man. They also told her that he could and had been ruthless when that was called for as well.

Barbara shivered in the cool morning air and burrowed deep under the covers. Marriage was not a simple affair. Not a simple affair at all. And this man she had married was an enigma. By turns he was kind and gentle and yet frightening. Had she not made her foolish wager she never would have met, never would have married this man. Just now, with all the mixture of emotions that were flowing through her, Barbara could not decide whether that would have been a blessing or a curse.

Eventually, perhaps around dawn, she slept.

On the far side of London, a man gambled with a vengeance. He threw the dice in his hand so hard that they bounced off the table and hit the floor. Angrily he rose from the table amidst loud protests, for he had been winning steadily. And still he walked away.

Winning didn't matter. Nothing mattered. Not when his enemy lay sound asleep on the other side of town. Farrington should have run from the church! Been forced to the altar, fighting every step of the way. Instead he had looked as well content as a man could be.

Lord Hurst, for that was who it was, clenched his fists until his nails bit into the palms of his hands. The only consolation, if there was one, was that Lady Barbara had looked as pale and frightened as anyone could have wished. And that gave him some satisfaction. But it was not enough. Farrington was the one who was supposed to suffer most. And he had looked far too well pleased with his choice.

Well that was a state of affairs that should not long continue, Hurst vowed. There were things he could do, rumors that could be spoken, which would rouse doubt in the most trusting husband's breast. And under the circumstances, how trusting could Farrington be to begin with?

Now a smile curved Lord Hurst's lips as he walked the mist-shrouded streets of London and headed for home. Perhaps something could be salvaged after all. And if Farrington began to distrust his blushing bride, perhaps something could be done to cause the bride to begin to distrust him, as well. And when one considered the matter, there was much, so much, to tell about Farrington!

Lord Hurst nodded to himself. Perhaps Farrington was content now, but how long would that last? There were ways, oh, yes, there were ways to alter matters. He would have his revenge. And then, perhaps then, Gerald's soul could rest and he, in turn, could find some peace.

Chapter 12

Damian stared at Barbara sleeping beside him. His wife. Why did the thought frighten him so? Perhaps because she was supposed to end his nightmares and instead they were worse than ever.

He shifted and stifled a curse. He wasn't used to sleeping with another person. How the devil was he to move about without disturbing her?

It would have been one thing, Damian thought irritably, if he could have taken Barbara into his arms, and in waking her made love to her. But he could not. Not after last night. He could not forget the way she had looked at him, the things he had said.

Never mind that they had made love, last night, after his nightmares. This was morning and Damian could not bring himself to do so again. Not when he could recall so clearly how vulnerable he had felt when she held him. Not when he could recall how close he felt to breaking.

Blast the woman! Impatiently he shoved aside the covers and got out of bed. Barbara stirred but did not wake and for that he was grateful.

He could not face her this morning. Not after what she had seen of him last night. After what they both had said. Of course, at the lodge—

Damian abruptly stopped, nearly overbalancing himself. The lodge? No. Instinctively, he shook his head. He could not take her there. He would come to hate Barbara if she saw him wake screaming from his dreams every night with no household of servants to stand buffer between them!

In horror, Damian dressed and fled the room. He didn't give a fig how poorly he tied his cravat. He wanted to be away before Barbara woke and stared at him with her disapproving, or worse, frightened eyes.

Barbara was not at all pleased to find Damian gone when she awoke. Mama had said this was how it was in well-regulated households. But she did not want a well-regulated household. She wanted one bound up in passion and love! And the very fact that Damian had deserted her so quickly on the morning after their wedding argued that it was a dream she would never possess.

With a hint of anger in her eyes, Barbara slipped from the bed and rang for her maid. She would dress as quickly as she could and then she would go in search of Damian. There were things they must talk about. Now. Before their marriage slipped into patterns neither one of them would be able to abide.

Even as she dressed, Barbara found herself making excuses for him. Perhaps Damian had wanted to rise early to make certain everything was ready for their journey. Perhaps he had not wanted to wake her. Perhaps he thought she would feel shy this morning and wish for privacy.

Her heart warmed at the thought of these excellent reasons for why Damian had not been at her side when she awoke. In much better spirits, Barbara went in search of her husband.

Ten minutes later, Barbara stared at Damian's majordomo. "What do you mean, Woodruff," she asked in an ominous tone, "that you don't know where Lord Farrington is?"

"His lordship went out and did not say where he was going or when he would return, milady," the majordomo replied, refusing to give way an inch or display any discomposure under his new mistress's stern gaze.

"But when? Why?" Barbara asked, bewildered.

Woodruff permitted himself a tiny shrug. "His lordship left over half an hour ago. As to where or why, I can give you no answer, milady. He did, however, tell me that he meant to return by dinner."

"Dinner?" Barbara echoed in angry disbelief. "But we were to—"

Abruptly Barbara caught herself. In spite of all her youthful rebellion, she was enough a Westcott to know she must not display certain behaviors, say certain things to a servant. So now, though it cost every ounce of willpower she had, Barbara forced a smile to herself and said, "Oh, that's right. I had forgotten. His lordship told me that there had been a change in plans. My mistake. Thank you, Woodruff, that is all."

If Woodruff had any doubts, he was too well-trained to betray them. Instead, he bowed deeply and said, "Very good, milady."

Barbara considered and discarded a dozen plans within a few minutes. She ought to go out herself. Not be here when Damian returned. That would teach him how she had felt. And yet, to do that would be to face the curious stares, the whispered comments, the pointed fingers of her friends. No, she could do nothing of the sort. She must merely wait here until he returned.

Except, of course, that Barbara never "merely" did anything. Her decision made, she decided to take up the reins of Damian's household. In the next hour she met with the cook and the housekeeper and made a few minor changes in the household routine. Changes that would not cause Damian or any of the servants any real discomfort, but which would signal to the staff her intent to keep firm control of the household now that she was mistress.

Barbara had just finished rearranging that night's

menu to her satisfaction when Woodruff announced, disapproval in every line of his body, "Lord Hurst has called, milady."

Excitement and embarrassment warred in Barbara's breast. Hurst had, after all, been privy to the disastrous wager, but on the other hand she had never known him to be boring, and she needed some amusement just now to divert her thoughts from her anger.

"Show him in," she said, ignoring Woodruff's patent disapproval.

"Yes, milady."

Moments later, Barbara held out both her hands to greet Lord Hurst. His eyes twinkled and he had a broad smile upon his face as he took her hands and kissed first one and then the other.

"You are in excellent looks, Lady Farrington," he said teasingly. "It is quite evident that marriage agrees with you!"

Barbara laughed. She could not help herself. It was so good to be teased again, and in such a way.

Encouraged, Lord Hurst went on, "I am putting myself in danger, you know, by coming here. Farrington and I have not been on the best of terms of late. But I could not stay away from my Lady Barbara! Besides, I knew it to be safe, having seen your husband enter his mistress's portal not twenty minutes since."

Barbara felt herself go stone cold at these words. Suddenly her laughter turned to ashes. Damian? At his mistress's? Already? Their marriage not even twenty-four hours old?

It was difficult to find words, difficult to make the sounds come from her throat, but she must. Lord Hurst was looking at her expectantly, waiting for some answer.

"Oh, of course!" Barbara said with a brittle little laugh. "Yes, Damian went to give the poor girl her congé. We talked about it last night, the two of us and decided it would be best."

"Of course, of course," Hurst repeated her words smoothly. Then he pursed his lips and added slyly, "Do you know, I have always admired a loyal wife. I only hope you have as loyal a husband, my dear. I should point out, however, that the warm embrace he gave her on the front steps might rather belie that pretty little tale you have just told me. I believe you, of course, but others might not."

Barbara went very pale and reached out a hand to brace herself on the nearest chair.

"Oh dear," Hurst said meekly, "now I've distressed you and I swear I did not mean to do so. I only wished to come and cheer you up and wish you the very best in your marriage. Whatever anyone else may say, I know that Lady Barbara is the one woman who will know how to take full advantage of her new freedom as a married lady."

He paused, then added shrewdly, "Just think! You are no longer bound by the rules that keep an unmarried girl in such shackles. You may do just as you wish! There are entertainments now open to you that just a week ago would have been beyond your reach. And should you like a list of them, I would be happy to oblige."

Barbara turned away. She was shaking, she could feel it. Nor was her voice altogether steady as she said, as coldly as she could manage, "I think you misjudge me, Lord Hurst. I mean to be a good wife to Lord Farrington."

Hurst spread his hands wide in a gesture of innocence. "Of course you do!" he said. "I do not doubt it. I simply meant that you would have more scope for your courage and daring than ever before."

"I think," Barbara said, still not able to look at him, "you had better leave, Lord Hurst. After all, Damian might return at any moment and that would be awkward for all three of us."

Hurst clenched his teeth together, but there was nothing he could do save retreat. He said all that was proper and pleasant, but the manner in which he jammed his hat upon his head as he left betrayed his anger.

Lady Farrington would regret her cavalier dismissal of him. Oh, yes, it was one more charge to the list he held against her. But by the time he was done, every one would be paid back in full, of that he was determined.

Behind him, Barbara was still shaking. She had read very well between the lines of what Lord Hurst had spoken. And she could not deny that her past behavior might have given him reason to believe that what he said was true.

But to her surprise she realized that she meant everything she had said to him. She would be a good wife to Damian, whatever the problems that arose between them at the start.

And yet, neither could Barbara forget what Lord Hurst had said about Damian. Was he with his mistress? Had he embraced her on the front steps? Had he forgotten already the vows he had taken only yesterday?

Suddenly Barbara laughed and shook her head. No, it was impossible! There was a detail, one little detail that made it all too much to swallow. She might believe that Damian had returned to his mistress, even this soon after his own marriage. But embrace her on the steps of her town house? Impossible! Damian would never be so thoughtless, so indiscreet.

Yes, but suppose the woman had embraced him? A tiny voice demanded.

Well, that might be possible, but Damian would have cut short the kiss as soon as it was begun. However brief a time she had known him, Barbara was certain of that. He might continue to visit his mistress, but he would not behave publicly in a way that would cause pain to his wife. His sense of honor would not permit it.

A little reassured, but still puzzled, Barbara sat down to wait for Damian. There were a number of books at hand and she chose one of them at random and opened it. Wherever he had been, whatever he had done, Barbara was determined that when Damian returned, he should not think she had only been sitting and waiting for him.

Damian was not, of course, at the house of his mistress. He did not have a mistress, though gossip accorded him any number of them. No, at the moment, he sat in The Fox and Hen and tried to forget where he had been this morning. At the same time, he tried to remember why he had been so certain Barbara could end his nightmares. It was absurd! A rude jest. Nothing could end these nightmares. Not wine, not whiskey, not brandy, and not even, it seemed, a wife.

He had behaved badly. Very badly, and Damian knew it. The question was, how was he to repair the damage before it grew any worse? He could not just leave matters as they stood. He could not do that to Barbara and he would not do it to himself.

Damian lifted his glass to drink from it again and then abruptly set it down. No. He would not find the answer in a bottle. He would have to tell Barbara about the dreams. And why they had driven him to speak to her as he had. It was still not too late to leave for the hunting box. And there, well, there perhaps they could learn to love one another, after all.

His decision made, Damian did not dawdle. Instead he rose to his feet and headed for the door. A hackney was quickly summoned and he was on his way home. Inexplicably his heart felt lighter. Perhaps Barbara could not stop the dreams, but he, Damian, could surely find a way to close the distance between the two of them and make this a good marriage in spite of how it had begun.

It was therefore with an eager step that Damian mounted the steps of his town house. Woodruff opened the door and it was at once evident that something had happened to overset the poor fellow.

"What?" Damian demanded tersely.

"Lord Hurst came to call," Woodruff answered as he took his lordship's hat and cloak.

Damian's eyes widened. "You denied him admittance, of course."

Woodruff hesitated. "He did not call to see *you*, milord," he said, stressing the word. "Lord Hurst called to see Lady Farrington. And claimed some urgency in doing so. I—I thought it best to let her decide."

"And she decided to see him?" Damian asked, his teeth clenched tightly at the end of the question.

Woodruff merely inclined his head in assent. Damian would have cursed fluently had he not been so conscious of the expectant way Woodruff stood waiting. Anything he said now would be all over the house, among the servants, within half the hour.

Damian forced himself to smile and yawn. "Oh yes, of course," he said lightly. "Her ladyship is well acquainted with the gentleman, I collect. Thank you, Woodruff, that will be all."

"But, sir, Lord Hurst!" Woodruff was moved to protest.

Damian hesitated, then clapped his majordomo on the shoulder. "It is all right," he said gently. "Though I much appreciate your concern on my behalf."

Woodruff sighed. "Yes, milord," he said and watched as Lord Farrington ascended the stairs toward his wife.

He had been with the family for many years and Master Damian, the wild one, had always been his favorite. He wasn't supposed to have favorites, but of course he did. And now Woodruff found that he very much hoped his lordship could find a way to bridge the gap between himself and his new bride.

For Woodruff discovered that he liked the lady, for all that she had been here only one day and had been disloyal enough to admit Lord Hurst to her company. No, in spite of everything, Woodruff wished both Lord and Lady Farrington happy.

Chapter 13

Damian paused in the doorway of the drawing room. Barbara sat curled up in a chair, reading one of his favorite books. His heart gave a little lurch at the sight. How often had he imagined coming home to just such a scene? Just such a beauty of a wife?

But in his daydreams, Damian thought wryly, his wife would have been in love with him. Loyal only to his interests, concerned only for his welfare, and disdainful of the company of other men. She would not have been a bride forced into marriage with him by some stupid wager. And she would never have dreamed of admitting, much less welcoming, Lord Hurst to his household.

But this was not a daydream. It was real life. And Damian must make the best of the circumstances in which he found himself. And if he was honest, perhaps some of the blame lay with him for having behaved as he had, both in the night and again this morning.

Damian took a step forward. "Barbara?" he said as gently as he could.

She looked up at him and for a moment there was only joy in her eyes. Then something akin to guilt, followed by a spark of anger, filled her eyes and when she spoke there was a patent constraint to her tones.

"Hello, Damian. I did not look to see you back so soon. Indeed, I did not know when to look for you. It was most disconcerting when the staff assumed I knew your plans and I did not."

That was not what Barbara had meant to say. Not what she had meant to say at all. She had meant to welcome him, to show him all the reason he should stay by her side. But she could not help herself. He had hurt her with his accusations last night, he had hurt her even more by his desertion, before she awoke, this morning.

Now Damian half turned away. "I told you I did not mean for us to live in one another's pockets," he replied in a cool, careless voice that tore through her. "And you should be grateful for that. For if I did, I should be asking you what you meant by admitting Lord Hurst to this house."

Barbara flinched as though struck, and then her anger rose to even greater heights. Biting off each word, she said, "Are the servants already telling tales, then? Do you mean to have them spy upon me, whenever you are gone? Am I to be forced to hide any behavior of which I think you might even possibly disapprove?"

Damian turned back to look at Barbara. His eyes were cold with his own rage. "The servants are, quite naturally, loyal to me and to my interests," he told her. "Most of them have been part of this household for many years. And they know Lord Hurst is not my friend."

Barbara flushed. Guilt and anger made her answer defensively, "Yes, but perhaps he is mine."

Damian slowly nodded. "Your friend," he said sardonically. "Lord Hurst was the cause of your foolish wager and of our forced marriage and yet you tell me that *perhaps* he is your friend?"

Barbara flushed. It was a hit. A palpable hit. She twisted her hands in her skirt and avoided his eyes. Her voice was small as she said, "I did not think of it in those terms, Damian, when he came. I remembered, instead, a friend who has often made me laugh and I admitted him so that he could offer me his congratulations on our marriage."

Damian stared at Barbara, his gaze burning into her. "Oh I have no doubt Lord Hurst was pleased by that," he said softly, so softly that he frightened her.

He stared at her a moment longer, then turned on his heel and left the room. As he walked down the hall, Damian was all but shaking. His intentions to repair the trouble between himself and Barbara were forgotten. Or if not forgotten, shoved to the background of his mind. Hurst. In his house. Welcomed by his wife.

He could not take Barbara to the hunting box. Not when he felt like this. Not when he felt such anger, such rage. He did not trust himself when he felt like this. Nor did he trust her. To understand when he needed understanding. To listen when he needed her to listen. To diffuse the anger that threatened to tear him apart.

It was not Barbara's fault that she was not what, or rather who, Damian had hoped she would be. But all the rational thinking in the world could not take away his disappointment. Or his rage.

No, they would stay in London. And Damian need not fear that he would hurt or truly frighten her. Not with so many people about.

As for Barbara, she stared after Damian's retreating back. That he would not be pleased she could understand, but it was more than mere displeasure she sensed. Was Damian so unhappy about their marriage? Was that why he held such a grudge against Lord Hurst?

With what might have been a tiny sob, Barbara picked up her book and tried to read again. It was a futile gesture, but the servants would not, she vowed, think her overset by this disagreement between Damian and herself.

And still she did not know if they were going to leave London or stay.

Lord Hurst, had he been privy to this conversation, would have been quite satisfied. As it was, he went straight from the Farrington household to his club. There he found a number of gentlemen willing to wager upon the new marriage and the likelihood that the irrepressible Lady Barbara would soon be looking about her for amusement.

The news of such wagers could not fail, Hurst concluded, to reach Lord Farrington's ears. And he would not be pleased. His step was light, therefore, as he then headed on a round of calls upon various ladies of his acquaintance. Ladies who would not fail to find it a delicious morsel of information when he told them that contrary to prior plans, the Farringtons had not left London for their honeymoon, but rather appeared to be finding entertainment, separate from one another, here in town.

Yes, and he would pretend to be all solicitous concern as he suggested that the new Lady Farrington would certainly be appreciative were these ladies so gracious as to pay her a morning call. They would leap at the chance to disconcert one of their own.

It was no wonder, then, that Hurst was in the best of spirits as he mounted the steps of the first house where he meant to call.

Sometime later that evening, and at a ball surrounded by his peers, Lord Hurst smiled and waved his hand carelessly. "Lady Barbara? Oh yes, I saw her this very morning. No, they have not left town," he said. "But then I believe this to be a marriage of convenience anyway, whatever they might say to the contrary. Certainly I have seen no evidence that her heart is engaged and we all know Farrington has none."

Lord Hurst paused and seemed to hesitate before he added, "Indeed, I should have said Lady Barbara looked almost lonely. But forgive me, I should not betray her confidences by saying so. And yet I cannot help but feel for her."

The group of young gentlemen clustered around Lord Hurst suddenly felt that they also could not help but feel for Lady Barbara, either. Poor girl, no doubt forced into this match by parents who had grown impatient to see her wed.

There was not one among this group who was not convinced she would have been happier with him. And not one who did not make a private vow to call upon her within the week to see if she wished for his company. After all, there was nothing exceptionable in that. And if there was, then let Lord Farrington say so.

Hurst watched the faces of the young men about him and felt a grim sense of satisfaction. He had no doubt that the word would spread and that there would be a steady parade of callers to see Barbara. And he knew Farrington well enough to suppose that such a circumstance would not be to his liking. If he called her to task for it, well, then there would be a furious row, for Barbara was not one to brook interference with her behavior.

Yes, all in all, it had been a productive day and evening, Hurst decided. Tomorrow he would do his best to arrange for Barbara to see Farrington engage several women of dubious reputation in private conversation.

Finally, when it was close to dawn, Hurst called on a lady he knew. At least she was a lady by birth. She was delighted to see him and listened with great interest to his plans and his proposal. By the time he was done, Lady Rathton was smiling very much like Lord Hurst.

"I shall be delighted," she purred, "to develop a

friendship with Lady Farrington. And to help you carry out your plans for her."

Lord Hurst would also have been delighted if he had been privy to the sight of Lord and Lady Farrington at the dinner table. They sat at opposite ends of the thing which had been meant for dinners of upward of twenty people. Now it held just the two of them in flickering candlelight.

It was not Damian's idea to have it so. He had asked that a place be laid to his right for Barbara. But she had chosen to countermand the order. Or so he thought. He was too proud to ask.

Nor did Barbara realize the confusion. She had simply come into the dining room to discover the places laid as they were and she took it as further proof that Damian wished her nowhere near him.

In the corner stood the footman who had changed the arrangement and told Woodruff it was by direct command. What he did not explain was that the command had come from Lord Hurst, accompanied by a hefty bribe. If anyone thought to talk to both his lord and her ladyship, his ruse would be discovered. But since the footman was being paid well to do what he did, he considered the risk worth taking. And he was too new to the household to have any loyalty to either Lord or Lady Farrington.

Still, no one was looking at him now. Instead they watched and listened with avid interest as Lord and Lady Farrington exchanged commonplaces. Even those who knew his lordship well did not guess the strength of the emotions he held in check. And none knew her ladyship well enough to guess at anything she felt.

Finally the servants were dismissed and Lord Farrington offered his arm to escort his wife from the room.

Barbara looked up at Damian, her hand trembling

slightly as she laid it on his arm. He was almost undone by the hint of something in her eyes that looked perilously like the start of tears.

As they walked down the hall to the drawing room she said softly, "Why are you so angry at me, Damian?"

"Angry? I?" he parried.

Barbara's grip tightened on his arm. "You know very well that you are. In part, I think, because I allowed Lord Hurst's company. But it is more than that. We were to have been on our way to your hunting lodge this morning and should have been safely there by now. Why did you change your mind?"

Damian hesitated. Perhaps he was a coward but he could not bring himself to talk about the dreams. Or his absurd belief that marrying her would bring an end to them. Instead he said lightly, "I thought you might find it boring there. That you would prefer to remain here, near your family, and in the midst of all the rounds of balls and such that are the Season."

Barbara slowly shook her head. "You are lying to me. I do not know why, but you are lying to me. You know very well that I do not care half so much for the Season as I do to make our marriage work."

Damian looked at her and tried very hard not to tremble himself. She saw so much, how could she not see clear through to his heart? He wanted to believe her, but some of the pain came back from last night. And from this morning.

"Do I?" he answered softly. "Then why did you admit my greatest enemy to this house?"

"I did not know he was," Barbara replied. "And you still have not told me why."

Now Damian halted and closed his eyes. When he opened them and looked down at her, there was something of the dark gleam she had seen the night before. It was also in his voice as he replied, just as he had this morning.

"Why do I need to tell you anything? You may not hate Lord Hurst for being the cause of a wager that forced us into marriage, but pardon me if I find it less easy a thing to forgive. Should that alone not have told you he was dangerous and to be avoided? At the theater, the night of our betrothal, you seemed to understand well enough what a rogue he was."

Barbara looked everywhere but at her husband's angry face. She wanted to make him understand. But how? Instinctively she knew he was in no mood to listen.

In a small, meek voice none of her sisters would have recognized, Barbara said, "Yes, Damian, but I was so lonely this morning. You were gone and I did not know where, and no one else was likely to call because they all thought us on our way out of London. It was foolish but surely not foolish enough to turn you against me like this?"

She paused, then in a stronger voice went on, "And besides, your anger must have been roused before you knew Lord Hurst had been here, or you would not have left the house so early, with not a word to me or the servants as to where you were going or why. Shall we discuss that?"

"I had my reasons," Damian replied stiffly.

Barbara stared at him and a sense of helplessness assailed her. His face was impassive, betraying nothing. She wanted desperately to ask him if he had gone to his mistress. But if there was one thing her mother had drilled into her head, it was that a wife must be silent on such matters. She must never pry into her husband's behavior in that respect.

But a thought had occurred to Barbara in the long hours since this morning. Had one night in her bed been sufficient to give Damian a disgust of her? Had he sensed her pleasure and been appalled by it? After all, her mother had told her that a lady should feel nothing. Nothing but a discomfort that could be dispelled only by thinking of the children one was going to have.

And what Barbara had felt was so far from discomfort that the comparison was ludicrous. It was the knowledge of just how unladylike she had been that in the end kept Barbara from speaking her thoughts aloud.

As for Damian, he thought he could bear this no longer. It was not fair to Barbara, not right, not sane. But he could not speak to her of his feelings or, God forbid, his dreams. He could not tell her what they meant to him, for that would have meant speaking of what he had seen and, far worse, what he had done during the years he had been away at war.

No, for her sake, Barbara must never know just what kind of monster she had married. Better to let her think him callous, than to saddle her with the understanding of what and who he truly was.

It was therefore with a mocking bow and a self-despising sneer that Damian turned to Barbara and said, "We will not agree on this, I see. Perhaps it would be best if you went up to bed and I retired to my study. You need not fear I shall disturb your sleep when I come to bed. It is not, I think, what either of us would want tonight."

And then he turned on his heel and strode away from her. Barbara half reached out to stop him, wanting to say that she did very much want him to disturb her sleep tonight. That she wanted his company. But it seemed pointless. He had, in every way possible, made it clear to her that he did not want hers.

Chapter 14

The advice Miss Tibbles had given Barbara, to make her own future, echoed in her ears and grew increasingly louder as the days passed and Damian continued to avoid her.

Not that Barbara was lonely or bored. Oh, no, there were far too many callers for that. Far too many ladies called to pay their respects to her and she could not help but see the curious and malicious intent behind their smiles. Only one or two, such as Lady Rathton, seemed genuinely friendly.

As for gentlemen, they called as well and that was even more of a trial for Barbara. All were as friendly as ever and the more disreputable hinted that were she ever to find herself lonely, they would be more than happy to keep her company.

No one seemed to believe her avowals that she meant to be a dutiful wife to her husband, not even Damian, who would often enter the salon to glare at the latest coterie of admirers who surrounded her.

And glower he did, for if Barbara was bewildered by all this attention, Damian was even more distraught. He ought to have been pleased, he told himself, that the *ton* had taken Barbara so much to its heart. But he was not. He recognized the knowing looks in their eyes and he did not like it. In spite of everything, he found within himself a growing desire to protect her from these predators of the *ton*.

Damian knew Barbara misunderstood his looks of

disapproval, but he could not bring himself to tell her the truth. Nor could he tell her that someone had sent him a private message warning him that his bride was not all that she seemed.

Damian chalked it up to malicious intent, but whose and why he did not know. He worried that Barbara would find herself hurt, for despite the fact that this was her second Season, she seemed so very young to him.

And so they grew increasingly far apart though Damian did, stubbornly, continue to share her bedroom.

In exasperation, Barbara finally sent for her sister Diana, who fortunately was making an extended stay in the city. Barbara welcomed her warmly when she came.

"I need your advice, Diana," she said bluntly.

Diana looked at her sister carefully. "What is wrong?" she asked.

Barbara told her everything. Well, almost everything. As Diana listened a suspicion occurred to her and she asked, "Are you having problems in the bedroom?"

"Diana!" Barbara exclaimed and sat bolt upright.

"Well? Are you?" Diana persisted, undaunted. "I can guess the advice Mama gave you and it was utterly wrong!"

Mortified, Barbara did not know which way to look. Diana did not wait for an answer but went on indignantly, "You should have come to me, Barbara. *I* would have advised you to enjoy yourself! I do not know Farrington but he has the reputation of a man who knows well how to please a woman and I should have told you to let him please you."

Barbara stared at her sister in astonishment. Cautiously she said, "But, Diana, Mama said I must not move. That I would give my husband a disgust of me if I showed the least sign of not disliking what he did."

Diana was all sympathy. She leaned forward. "And so you followed her advice? That is what has caused the problem between you and Lord Farrington?"

"No! That is, I did not do as Mama advised," Barbara blurted out, "and now I fear Farrington has taken me in disgust!"

Diana leaned back and laughed. She did not mean to, but it was impossible to help herself. At Barbara's look of outrage, Diana hastily tried to explain herself. "It is far more likely that Farrington would be delighted to find a willing partner in his bed," she said bluntly.

"But he is not," Barbara replied.

Diana reached out and put a sympathetic hand over Barbara's. "I wish I knew what to tell you. Surely it is some misunderstanding. After all, he chose to marry you and he could not, recluse or not, have thought you a shy, shrinking sort of girl, the sort Mama told you to be."

And indeed, Diana's words conjured up an image of that night at the inn. No, Damian could not have mistaken her for a shy, shrinking sort of girl at all. But he had married her out of a sense of honor, Barbara reminded herself silently. Not out of love or true desire.

Just then there was a sound at the doorway of the room. Both Westcott sisters turned to see Damian. He came forward reluctantly. As though good manners, and not his own desire, prompted him to do so.

"Your Grace," Damian said, bowing deeply to Diana.

"Lord Farrington. Will you join us?" Diana asked. "We had no chance to talk at the wedding and I wanted to tell you how pleased I am to see my sister happily settled."

Damian hesitated. He found himself oddly yearning to do just that. To pretend this was a conventional marriage and that he was on excellent terms with his wife's family. But he was too well aware of how far from the truth that was.

Still, he made the attempt. "Thank you, Your Grace," Damian said as he sat beside Barbara. "How long will you and Berenford be in London?"

Diana waved a hand carelessly. "Oh, a few weeks, perhaps. It is an excellent chance to see family. Indeed, I came to ask if the both of you would like to make up a party to go to the theater tonight. Annabelle and Winsborough and Jeremy and I will be there as well."

He meant to refuse, but that odd yearning made Damian answer instead, "We shall be delighted."

Then, afraid he would betray himself if he stayed any longer, Damian rose swiftly to his feet as he added, "I shall look forward to seeing you all then. You may arrange everything with Barbara. I must go."

Then, before either lady could say a word, Damian left. Finally Diana found her voice. "That was kind of him to accept and rude of him to leave us so abruptly," she said.

Barbara looked down at her hands. "Just so have I come to expect a mixture of consideration and brusque indifference from Damian and I haven't the faintest notion how to alter that."

Impulsively she leaned forward. "Tell me, Diana, how do you and Berenford manage to remain so warm toward one another? For it is unmistakable in the way you look at one another. In the way you touch one another, scarcely without thinking. The way there is a caress in his voice when he speaks to you. That is what I would like to have with Damian."

Diana colored. How could she tell Barbara about the rides she and Jeremy were wont to take out on their estate? The private jests, the pretense that Jeremy was a groom? Instead she tried to divert Barbara's attention.

"You must not allow yourself to fall in the megrims," Diana said. "Go shopping. Visit friends. Enjoy the privileges of being a wife. If you hang on Lord Farrington's sleeve you may give him a disgust of you. But if he sees you out and about he may very well come in search of you."

It was well meant. Diana could scarcely know or guess that it was the worst possible advice she could have given Barbara. Or that the evening at the theater would lead to disaster.

No one seeing Lord Farrington dance attendance upon his wife at the theater that night could have guessed the emotions seething within his breast. The Duke and Duchess of Berenford were all that was kind to him as were Lord and Lady Winsborough. What, then, was the problem?

The problem, Damian told himself as he clenched and unclenched his fists in the shadows, was that Barbara had far too many smiles for far too many gentlemen who waved to her from other boxes. And that she carried a posy and fan given to her by some other admirer and not him.

It did not occur to Damian to ask Barbara about the fan and posy. If he had he would have discovered that *she* was under the impression that both had come from him.

But that would have been the sensible thing to do and Damian's emotions were far too deeply engaged for him to be sensible at this particular moment. Therefore every time she pointedly held up the posy or fan and smiled at him, Damian felt as though she were slapping him in the face.

Barbara, however, was in excellent spirits. She positively glowed. All could not possibly be lost, after all, if Damian was sending her posies and fans. It was just like him, she thought, to couch his notes so discreetly and have them delivered rather than give her the gifts himself.

Well, if Damian could make such a generous gesture, then she, too, could make advances to him. Perhaps all that was needed was for them to rekindle a little of the feelings that had been born that night at the inn.

So Barbara flirted with Damian and he silently gnashed his teeth at what seemed to be her intolerable insults toward him.

"This is such a delightful fan," Barbara said, tapping his elbow with it. "And the carving in the ivory so intricate! Look, I can see trees and people and even little animals. However do they do it, I wonder."

"I cannot," Damian said grimly, "for the life of me imagine."

Barbara tried again. She sniffed at her posy. "Do you not think these the most delightful blossoms?"

"I think the scent is going to make me sneeze," Damian retorted as she held it out toward him.

"Oh. Well, in that event, I shall keep it farther from you," Barbara said.

She hesitated. Something was very wrong here in Damian's response. He appeared to be intent upon the play and yet she did not think that was why he was so impatient with her attempts to express how much she liked his gifts. For the first time it occurred to her that perhaps he had not, after all, been the one to send them to her.

By intermission, Damian was wondering how the devil he could gracefully leave the theater. Barbara was determined to unravel the mystery and repair this new damage between them. Her sisters and their husbands were intent on helping the couple in whatever way they could.

No one in the box, therefore, was pleased when the door opened and a flock of gentlemen intruded, led by Lord Hurst. A cry went up as one of the gentlemen recognized Barbara's posy.

"There, Harry, I'll have that crown from you, for I told you she would carry it tonight, didn't I?"

As Damian started to rise to his feet, another shout went up from another gentleman. "Yes, but, George, *you* owe *me* two crowns for it is *my* fan she carries!"

Barbara sat stock-still and wished the floor could open up and swallow her. Damian was furious, but his concern was all for Barbara. He had to do something, and swiftly, or by tomorrow morning her name would be bandied all over London.

Damian turned to her and said with a yawn, "I thought it would be more amusing, my love, to see the young puppies tumble over one another to earn your attention. But you were right, it is a dead bore. I am sorry I persuaded you to carry these tokens. I wonder, should we admit that you chose the posy and fan quite at random?"

Instantly there was silence, dead silence, in the box. The two young men in question went white with mortification. Barbara's own face was pale but she followed his lead.

"You are too cruel, Damian. These gentlemen were kind to send me their gifts. How can you roast them like this?"

"Because," Damian said, a hint of steel in his voice, "I would not wish them to be so foolish as to confuse *your* kindness with encouragement."

"No, no, nothing of the sort," George said hastily.

"Quite right," the other gentleman agreed. "No impertinence meant, Farrington. Quite understand she's your wife and most devotedly so."

Even as they spoke, the two gentlemen were backing toward the door of the box. Lord Hurst stepped aside to let them, to let all the young gentlemen, escape. Finally only he was left.

"That was neatly done," he said to Barbara approvingly. "They might even have believed you, young puppies that they are. I, of course, understand only too well the care you must take with Lord Farrington here at your side. Even I have heard of his skill with pistols."

A hiss of indrawn breath warned Barbara that Hurst had touched a sore point with Damian. She could only wonder what it was. She tried to put Hurst in his place before matters became any worse.

Lightly she said, "You are roasting me, Lord Hurst, and I do not think it kind of you."

"Kind?" he asked, pressing a hand to his breast. "But, Lady Farrington, what would lead you to expect kindness from me? Surely experience has taught you to expect the reverse?"

This last was said with a malicious twist to the voice and a sideways glance at Barbara's sisters, who were watching Hurst with puzzled faces.

For a moment, matters hung in the balance. Damian wanted badly to call Hurst out. Had he not been here, in the theater, with his wife and her sisters at his side, he might well have done so. But he could not.

Instead Damian said lightly, "No one, Hurst, would expect you to be anything other than what you are."

It was an insult, decidedly an insult. Now it was Lord Hurst's hands that clenched into fists. The people in the box held their collective breaths but Hurst, after a long moment's hesitation, laughed. Carelessly. And said, "You are trying to provoke me, Farrington, but I shall not allow it. You shall not do to me what you did to my brother."

And then, before Damian could reply, Hurst turned on his heel and left the box. Barbara turned to her husband to ask what Hurst could have meant and saw that he was white as a sheet. Her sisters seemed to notice as well, for Annabelle pulled a tiny vinaigrette from her reticule and snapped open the lid. Instantly the smell of hartshorn filled the area and Damian turned toward her.

In acid tones he said, "I wish, Lady Winsborough, that if you feel overcome and must use a restorative, you would at least have the courtesy not to wave it all about so that the rest of us must smell that abominable odor as well."

Lord Winsborough bristled. Barbara put a hand on Damian's arm. Even the Duke of Berenford looked as though he meant to rise from his seat. It was Diana, the Duchess of Berenford, who outfoxed them all.

With a brittle laugh that must have looked genuine from the distance of any other box, she said, "Why, Lord Farrington, you are drawing all eyes to us! Surely that is *not* what you wish? Nor you, Lord Winsborough or Jeremy? Clearly Lord Farrington has been put out of sorts by Lord Hurst, but surely none of us need make it worse?"

In the silence, Damian managed to smile. It was a false smile, of course, but it was sufficient to fool those too far away to have heard any of the exchanges.

"You are right, of course," Damian said. "My apologies, Lady Winsborough."

Annabelle smiled warmly at him. "None needed, Lord Farrington. I quite understand."

Perhaps Annabelle did, but Barbara was furious. How dare he insult her sister? Particularly when Annabelle was only trying to help? Barbara made herself smile, but the smile did not reach her eyes.

When they were set down at home by the Duke and Duchess of Berenford, Damian was mentally congratulating himself on having salvaged what might have been a disastrous evening. Not knowing Barbara well, he took her smiles at face value and therefore was unprepared for the tirade she unlashed upon him the moment they were alone in the drawing room.

"How dare you treat my sister in such a way?" Barbara demanded.

"I have already apologized," Damian replied in soothing tones. "She forgave me."

Barbara's eyes narrowed. She began to pace back and forth. "Well I have not! Annabelle is too sweet-tempered for her own good. Unfortunately for you, sir, I am very different. I do not forget an insult to me or to my family! I do not forgive simply because someone prettily begs my pardon!"

Damian tried to be patient. He crossed his arms and said mildly, "What do you require, to forgive someone?"

Barbara stopped her pacing and looked directly at Damian. "Atonement," she declared.

He tried to make a joke of it. "What? Should I send her flowers? A pretty fan, perhaps? Lord Winsborough would be within his rights to call me out!"

Barbara went red, then very pale. "How dare you?" she whispered, shaking with rage. "You know very well I thought the flowers and fan came from you!"

"No I didn't," Damian promptly replied.

It was an error. Barbara threw the offending articles to the floor and stamped on them. She was blinking back tears as she flung back her head, tilted her chin into the air, and said defiantly, "Well, you ought to have known! You ought to have known that I would never have offered you such an insult as to carry another man's offerings, now that I am married to you. But if you have so little faith in me, then perhaps there is no hope for our marriage after all."

Dismayed, Damian reached out toward her. But Barbara had already fled toward the doorway of the drawing room. She ran upstairs and he could hear her feet light upon the stairs and the sobs that racked her as she ran.

Damian started to follow but he then made his second error. He decided to give her time to calm down, time to think. He had, after all, no experience with the married state or he would never have done such a foolish thing.

Several drinks later, Damian went upstairs, congratulating himself upon his tact. Until he got to the bedroom door and discovered that Barbara had locked him out.

Damian felt a sense of disbelief. He tried the door twice. Then he knocked softly, thinking Barbara might have locked it by mistake. Then he began to think of ways to dismantle the door, since breaking it down would no doubt bring all the servants running.

The trouble was, of course, that Damian never had dismantled a door before. He thought he might know how to do so if he had the proper tools, but what were the proper tools? That was something his education had neglected to teach him.

Damian turned and entered the adjoining bedroom, where the door to his dressing room, which was between the two bedrooms, stood open. His valet Phillips was waiting, an expression of resignation on his face.

The valet looked at the other door, then at Damian. "Locked," he said succinctly.

He looked at Phillips sharply. "Where are the keys?" Damian demanded.

"I should think," the valet said cautiously, "that her ladyship is in possession of them. Otherwise I cannot think she would dare to do as she has done. But the spares, if any, would be in the kitchen, I suppose."

For a moment, Damian and Phillips stared at one another, then they moved as one. Within minutes they were in the kitchen. All the keys had been removed. When? Damian didn't know and he didn't care. He turned to Phillips. "Are there any others?" he asked.

"Perhaps Woodruff would know?" the valet suggested delicately. "In any event, he is the most discreet person to ask."

Damian nodded. "Fetch him!" he said, suddenly realizing he hadn't the faintest notion where Woodruff disappeared to once he went below stairs.

But there was no need to fetch Woodruff. He had heard the noise and now he appeared in the kitchen. "Is there any way I may be of service?" he asked, hiding his surprise. "Is your bellpull out of order, my lord?"

Through gritted teeth Damian asked, "Keys, Woodruff. Where are the spare keys?"

Woodruff peered faintly at the spot where the spare keys should have hung. "I don't know, my lord," he said, puzzled. "Which keys were you looking for?"

Damian went red then white. Could matters have become any more humiliating? Was he really going to have to admit that his wife had locked him out?

Fortunately, Phillips came to the rescue. He yawned and said, "A wager, Woodruff, it was a wager, I collect. His lordship needs to see and count all the spare keys. Run along and fetch them posthaste, if you please."

But this was too much for Woodruff. Jealous of the valet, he was not about to allow himself to be ordered about by the paltry fellow. In an austere voice he said, "I shall look for the spare keys in the morning, my lord. I am certain they will turn up. Perhaps her ladyship has them, for some reason. Have you tried asking her?"

Damian fled the kitchen, followed closely by Phillips, who paused only long enough to abuse the majordomo roundly. Upstairs in the dressing room both men stared at the locked door for a long time. Both men cautiously tried the handle.

Finally Phillips said, "I could make up a cot for you in here, my lord. No one need know."

Damian hesitated, then nodded.

Phillips silently shuddered at the banked rage in his lordship's eyes. He wouldn't want to be Lady Farrington in the morning, not by a long chalk he wouldn't.

Chapter 15

Damian awoke early, never really having fallen soundly asleep. He was sore from the cramped positions he had contorted himself into to fit on the cot. And he was most definitely in a foul mood.

His first act was to test the door. Still locked. So Barbara had not regretted, even in the middle of the night, her act of rebellion. Damian once again resisted the impulse to break down the door.

Let her think he didn't care. Let her think anything she liked so long as she never guessed how profoundly the separation hurt him. Perhaps her presence had not been enough to end the nightmares, but Damian had come to want, to need her softness beside him when he woke afterward. To know that she was there, within reach.

No, let the shrew but guess how important she was to him and she would hold it over his head like a dagger. As his father and brothers had done for all the years he was growing up.

His decision made, Damian washed and dressed in the dressing room. That was, after all, he thought ironically, what it was meant for. And then he padded softly downstairs, careful not to wake Barbara. Let her wonder what his reaction had been, let her try to guess where he had gone, let her fear what he would do when he returned.

* * *

It was less than an hour later when Barbara awoke. She felt a sense of profound desolation as she reached for Damian and remembered that she had locked him out of their room. To be sure, she still felt she had cause, but her treacherous heart missed him.

Barbara rose and unlocked the door before the servants could discover what she had done. And as she dressed, it was with a sense of anticipation, wondering what Damian would say to her this morning, wondering why he had not simply broken down the door last night. She would not admit, even to herself, that she had felt more than a twinge of disappointment that he had not. Nor would she admit that she had worked out in her mind just how she would have faced him bravely, defiantly, and in the end, lovingly.

Now the scene would have to be enacted over the breakfast table and that was not nearly so satisfactory a scenario. Particularly as, Barbara discovered when she went downstairs, that Damian had already quit the house.

Incensed, Barbara had to force herself to sit and eat instead of pacing angrily. Did he not care? Did he think so little of her that a night locked out of the bedroom was of no importance to him? Well, it was not to be borne! She would make him look at her, speak to her, do something to show that he was not entirely indifferent!

With a grim look in her eyes, Barbara sent a note round to Lady Rathton, accepting her offer to take her shopping. Lady Rathton was the one woman of her acquaintance, after all, who could be counted upon to encourage just what Barbara had in mind.

A return note expressed that lady's delight and a promise to be round shortly with her carriage to take Barbara up and show her the best, the most unusual shops in London. Everything out of the common way would be shown to her and Barbara was to come prepared to indulge her fancy.

It was only a pity that Damian was not there to see the expedition embark. Lady Rathton was all kindness as she greeted Barbara. Barbara was all delight at the comfort of Lady Rathton's equipage. And when that lady pooh-poohed the notion of calling at the modiste Lady Westcott had always patronized for her daughters, Barbara was more than happy to listen to her advice.

"You are a married woman now," Lady Rathton said knowledgeably, "and ought to take full advantage of your new position. You need no longer be an insipid miss, you may be as daring as you choose. I have it! We shall go to Madame Dubrovny."

Madame Dubrovny! Barbara had long admired her daring designs. The notion that she could now indulge her taste for them was a very nice one indeed. Particularly when she could not help but realize how likely Damian was to disapprove of them.

It was a short distance to the right address and within minutes they entered the shop. Upon hearing Lady Farrington's name, Madame Dubrovny instantly appeared and waited upon the new customer herself. She guided Barbara and Lady Rathton into a private room, gave orders for hot chocolate to be brought, and sat down to discuss with Barbara what her current needs might be.

"For the first time in my life, madame," Barbara said, "I may choose my dresses to suit me. I will not wear anything insipid or pastel or with a neckline up to here. I wish to be beautiful, to be daring, to have all eyes turn to me when I enter a room," she concluded, not realizing how directly she was repeating Lady Rathton's words in the carriage.

Madame Dubrovny rose to her feet and circled Barbara. She exchanged a look with Lady Rathton and then slowly she nodded her head.

"Yes, you have the figure for it," Madame Dubrovny agreed. "And the fire is in your eyes. I think we might very well dress you so that you are the envy of all the other ladies in London. But you must put yourself entirely in my hands, you know," she warned.

Barbara hesitated. After all, one reason for coming here instead of to her mother's modiste was so that she should not be bullied.

As though she sensed Barbara's concern, Lady Rathton leaned close and said, "It will be such a lark, I assure you! Madame Dubrovny will trick you out in feathers so fine you will turn heads and in dresses of which your mother will not approve."

Barbara turned to Lady Rathton, who nodded slowly as Barbara's eyes grew wide. Dresses Mama would disapprove of? Turn heads? Oh yes!

"I am yours to dress as you see fit," she told Madame Dubrovny.

Barbara did not see the satisfied glance exchanged between Madame Dubrovny and Lady Rathton. Even if she had she would have assumed it was merely because the two had the sort of discreet arrangement where Lady Rathton steered friends toward Madame Dubrovny and in consequence Madame gave Lady Rathton a reduction in the cost of her gowns.

Two hours later, Barbara was even more satisfied than when she had come in. She had seen and approved gowns in every possible color that would suit her. For Madame Dubrovny was quite insistent that Barbara should wear bold colors, not pastel, and nothing that did not enhance her complexion. Since this suited Barbara perfectly, there was no discord.

Lady Rathton chose one or two ensembles herself, but as she told Barbara teasingly, "This is your day, not mine. I shan't do anything to distract Madame's attention from you. Oh, how I shall enjoy watching all of London fall at your feet in admiration when they discover that far from being an insipid schoolgirl, you are a lady of sophistication!"

This did indeed give Barbara a moment of hesitation. All of London did already know she was far from an insipid schoolgirl. She had spent her first Season and this one, until the day after her disastrous wager, doing her best to prove to the *ton* that she was not. How was it that Lady Rathton did not know her story?

It was as though Lady Rathton could read Barbara's mind. At that moment she tapped her chin thoughtfully and said, "Not, mind you, that I think anyone ever did mistake you for an insipid schoolgirl. A headstrong one, perhaps, but not insipid. Now, however, now they will see you as a grown woman and one of great daring and beauty. You will have an endless string of admirers, I assure you."

But she didn't want a string of admirers, Barbara thought sadly. She wanted Damian to love and admire her. Barbara must have said this aloud for Madame Dubrovny snorted and said, "A husband is much more likely to love and admire his wife if other men do as well. One would not wish the fools to take one for granted."

Barbara smiled hesitantly. Was that true of Damian? Perhaps. In any event, it was so nice to be able to dress in the colors she loved. And to be able to choose dresses that made her, at last, feel grown up.

When they finally left Madame Dubrovny's establishment, the coachman was still patiently waiting. Lady Rathton directed the driver to Gunther's for ices.

There Lady Rathton looked at Barbara and said, "Do you know, I have the oddest sense that you would make an excellent whipster?"

Barbara looked up at her. "Oh, I am," she said. "At home I was used to tool a carriage about whenever I wished. But here in London it is not allowed."

"Not for a young girl," Lady Rathton agreed, tilting her head to one side, "but then we have already agreed you are going to prove to London that you are now a woman all grown, have we not?"

"Yes," Barbara agreed warily.

"I don't suppose your husband has yet bought you a proper equipage?" Lady Rathton asked thoughtfully.

"No. That is, I do not think he has," Barbara replied hesitantly.

Lady Rathton shook her head. "Depend upon it, if he had, he would have told you so at once. Men can never resist telling a woman how generous and wonderful they are. But that is just as well."

Barbara blinked. "It is?" she asked even more warily.

"Oh, certainly," Lady Rathton replied. "If Lord Farrington had bought you a carriage you may depend upon it that it would have been a boringly safe and respectable sort of thing with not the least excitement to it. Now I, on the other hand, propose that we acquire for you, if you have the funds, of course, a proper sporting thing. Indeed, I have it! I know of a high-perch phaeton and a matching pair available without requiring the slightest delay!"

Barbara's own eyes began to sparkle. "A high-perch phaeton? I should love such a thing above half! But how? We are not allowed into Tattersall's to choose a pair."

Lady Rathton put a hand over Barbara's. "Leave it all to me, I pray you," she said. "I know how it can be arranged in a trice. You shall have your carriage and horses before the next week is out."

"Could you arrange such a thing?" Barbara asked, scarcely daring to hope.

"Oh, I can," Lady Rathton assured her. "And I only ask in return that you promise that you will take your first race with me."

"Race?"

Lady Rathton tapped her chin, "Twice around the

park, I should think, and neither of us to overturn either ourselves or any other carriage."

"But isn't that improper?" Barbara asked, feeling a twinge of alarm.

Lady Rathton delicately shrugged a shoulder. "No doubt there are those who would think so, but I took you for a daring creature. It is one of the things I like best about you. Was I mistaken?"

"No, no," Barbara answered hastily. Then, defiantly, she added, "I am quite daring enough for anything."

Lady Rathton smiled. "Good," she said. "I knew I could not be mistaken in you. I shall arrange for it at once. I tell you, you shall have your new carriage and horses before the next week is out."

Now Barbara did understand that to race in the park with Lady Rathton in a high-perch phaeton would be sufficient to put her beyond the pale. And had Damian behaved with even the slightest modicum of sense when she returned home, Barbara would have sent round a note canceling her order for the carriage and the proposed match.

But Damian had unfortunately sought the advice of a friend who was not leg-shackled, had never fallen in love, and believed that because he had survived the parson's trap he knew precisely how one ought to handle a woman. If only Damian had been wise enough not to listen!

He was waiting, hands on hips, when Woodruff directed Barbara, with a hint of sympathy in his voice, to the drawing room.

"Well, you have certainly been gone long enough," Damian said the moment she was in the room and had closed the door behind her.

Barbara tossed her hat and gloves on the sofa before she answered, "I am surprised you even noticed, the way you disappear so early and return so late."

Damian strode over to Barbara and took her by the shoulders. "I will not have it!" he said.

"You will not have what?" she countered.

He gave her a little shake. "This levity. This irreverence. This defiance of me as your husband!" Damian all but roared.

Barbara lifted her eyes and met his coolly. She made a moue that might have been either distaste or amusement. "Oh? And how do you propose to stop me?" she demanded.

Damian let go of her shoulders and crossed his arms. There was a look of smug triumph on his face as he said, "I have had the lock to the bedroom doors removed."

Barbara might have pointed out that if they ever did patch up their differences, he might regret doing so. Particularly if an unwary maid walked in too early one morning. But she did not. Instead she laughed. She laughed at Damian and said, "You are a fool if you think that will do any good."

A puzzled look crossed Damian's face. This wasn't how it was supposed to go. That wasn't what Barbara was supposed to say. She was supposed to beg his pardon and promise never to try to lock him out again.

Barbara turned on her heel, plucked her hat and gloves off the sofa, and marched from the room. Damian followed.

"Where have you been?" he demanded.

"Out."

"Doing what?"

"Shopping."

"What did you buy?"

Now Barbara paused on the stairs and turned to face Damian, conscious of the fascinated servants listening behind nearby doors. She smiled a seraphic smile at him.

"Why, you will just have to wait and see, *my dearest*

Damian," she all but purred. "I would not, will not, ruin the surprise by telling you."

And Damian, equally conscious of nearby ears, could do nothing but grind his teeth and continue to follow her up the stairs. Which he did, allowing her to move no more than scant inches ahead of him.

In the bedroom he reached for her, still following his friend's abominable advice. Barbara neatly evaded him and tugged on the bellpull before he could stop her.

Then, sweetly, she said, "Are you going to lock the door before my maid comes? Ah, but I forgot, you can't. You had the lock removed."

"I shall send her away," Damian said, taking another step toward Barbara.

"And then I shall scream the moment she is gone," Barbara countered, still very sweetly, as she moved swiftly out of his way. "I have no doubt the servants will all come running to discover what is amiss."

She was absolutely right and they both knew it. Damian came to a halt. He would not pursue her further. Not now, at any rate. He bowed to Barbara as though to an opponent with whom he had just fenced.

"Until this evening," he said, and in his words were both a promise and a threat.

Chapter 16

When evening came, Barbara went upstairs ahead of Damian. He let her go, telling himself that in any event her maid would be there, helping her to undress. If he felt a twinge of unease, he suppressed it by pouring himself another glass of brandy.

To be sure, his friend's advice had not worked all that well as yet, but perhaps Barbara merely needed time to grasp the sense of what he was trying to do. In any event, he was determined to show her who was master in this house.

Damian went upstairs full of confidence. Confidence which was shattered when he realized the bedroom was empty. Puzzled, he walked into his dressing room and found Phillips waiting for him.

"My lord, shall you prepare for bed now?" the valet asked expectantly.

Clearly Phillips had no suspicion that anything was wrong and Damian decided to keep it that way. "Yes, of course," he answered.

Damian kept an ear tilted toward the bedroom, fully expecting to hear Barbara return to the bedroom at any moment. She did not.

When he was ready for bed, Damian thanked Phillips and dismissed him, suppressing the impulse to ask him if he knew where Lady Farrington might be.

When he was finally alone, Damian searched the bedroom, but he found not a clue as to where Barbara had gone. The dress she had been wearing earlier that evening now hung in the wardrobe. Nor did he think she was missing any other of her dresses. Though how he could be certain was another question entirely. Still, he told himself stoutly, if Barbara had decided to run away, surely she would have done so earlier in the day.

After making certain there were no servants lingering about, Damian padded down the hallway, peering into one bedroom after another. It took some time, for all the doors were unaccountably closed.

Finally he came to one he could not open and with disbelief and rage Damian realized that Barbara had found a way to lock him out, after all!

He knocked on the door softly, reluctant to have any of the servants know what had happened. There was no answer. He called out her name.

"Barbara, open this door! Right now. Or I shall not be answerable for my actions," he warned.

Still no answer. Damian pounded louder, not caring anymore who heard him. He was going, he vowed, to make her open that door.

"Go away, Damian," Barbara replied coolly from the other side when he stopped. "I am not coming out tonight and you may as well accept that fact."

Through clenched teeth Damian said, "Tomorrow you will regret this, Barbara."

"Perhaps," she answered sweetly, "but this is tonight. Pleasant dreams, Damian."

Fury flowed all through him. But there was not a thing he could do. Not unless he wanted to break down the door. And Damian refused to do so. There were too many other doors, after all, that she could hide behind. No, he simply made his plans. Tomorrow all the locks throughout the house would be removed.

Silently Damian padded back to the bedroom and the empty bed. Pointlessly, he tried to sleep.

* * *

The next morning, Damian rose early and sent for the locksmith again. Not by a jot did that fellow betray his astonishment at being told that all the locks from all the doors must be removed. Nor did any of the servants dare ask about the master's latest start.

Barbara betrayed not the least sign of dismay either. Damian looked at her with a triumphant smile, daring her to counter this move. She merely smiled in return.

He should have been warned by that smile but then Damian had never encountered a creature quite like Barbara before. There were, it seems, many ways in which his education had been lacking.

Evening came and this time Damian followed Barbara upstairs. Propriety dictated, however, that he remove to the dressing room and the presence of Phillips to disrobe while her maid helped Barbara do the same.

He was as quick about the business as possible but with one thing and another she was done before him. And when Damian entered the bedroom he discovered Barbara once again was gone.

Puzzled, he started down the hallway. Whatever could she be thinking? There were no locks on the doors. Confused, Damian checked each room systematically. He found her in the bedroom at the end of the hall, opposite the one she had used the night before.

Damian threw open the door and advanced mercilessly on the bed, where Barbara watched him without the least trace of fear in her eyes. She sat cross-legged on top of the covers and waited for him to reach her.

That only inflamed Damian's temper even more. "You are coming back to bed," he said, grasping her wrist.

Barbara did not move. If the tug on her wrist was

painful, she did not betray it. Instead she watched him silently. After a moment, Damian let go of the wrist and scooped her up.

"You are my wife," he said, grimly, "and as such you are going to share my bed."

Still Barbara did not answer. Not even when Damian marched down the hall with her. Not even when he shut the door behind him with his foot. Not even when he dumped her on the bed and began to untie the belt of his robe.

No, Barbara watched him quite calmly, knowing with utter certainty that however angry he was, Damian would not force her.

Suddenly Damian groaned and turned away as he came to the same realization himself. He wanted a willing wife, not one who would hate him for what he did to her. And he knew Barbara was capable of passion. Doggedly he was determined to settle for nothing less.

Almost, at the look of pain in his eyes, Barbara relented. But then she immediately hardened her heart again. This marriage would be no true marriage unless Damian accepted her as his wife in ways other than the bedroom. He must, he would show her consideration. He would show her that he cared or she would turn only a cold shoulder to him! Determinedly Barbara turned her back on him.

Damian sat on the bed and gently stroked her shoulder and back with the tip of his fingers. "Come, Barbara, can we not make things up?" he asked coaxingly.

"No."

"Not even if I kiss you here? And here? And here?"

Dear Lord, he was much too persuasive with his kisses! Barbara hastily turned onto her back and stared rigidly up at the ceiling.

Now he stroked her cheek and down her throat to

caress the top of her breasts. "What about this?" he asked softly. "Or this?"

He kissed her then, full on the lips, and it took every ounce of self-control Barbara possessed to keep her own mouth still. Even so tears ran down her cheeks. Was she going to destroy both of them with her stubbornness?

But Damian mistook the reason for her tears. He saw them and drew back horrified. "Barbara!" he whispered. "I did not mean . . . That is . . . Don't cry, I shan't force you," he told her urgently.

She turned away, unable to either stop the tears or explain them to him. Just as she was about to concede everything, Damian rose from the bed and padded toward his dressing room.

From the doorway there he said, roughly, "Go to sleep. I don't force children. When you are ready to be a wife and not a spoiled child, then maybe you'll remember that there was a time you did not find my embrace quite so distasteful as you evidently do right now."

Barbara burst into louder tears as the door between the rooms was shut with a slam. By the time he returned, some hours later, she had exhausted herself into a deep sleep. Damian watched her bitterly. He climbed into bed beside his wife and lay awake long into the night.

That was how it was to be for several nights in a row. In the day he and Barbara were too angry with one another to be civil. At night, every night, she would hide in one or another of the bedrooms and he would have to hunt her down. For Damian was stubbornly adamant that she should continue to share his bed.

Once he did carry her back to their bed, Damian would do his best to seduce her. And Barbara would do her best to remain cold. Apparently she was a better actress than she could have guessed for Damian always gave up in exasperation and went into his dressing room until he was certain she had fallen asleep.

It was a situation that was satisfactory to neither of them. As the days passed, lack of sleep and frustration made them both increasingly short-tempered.

It was a disaster and they both knew it. They were both, however, equally determined that it was the other who would first make amends. The other who would first cry surrender. And given that it was Barbara and Damian, any fool could have predicted it wasn't going to happen.

Chapter 17

Lack of sleep may have been the reason it took Damian a moment or two to realize what it was he was seeing one morning, a week or so later, when he emerged from the town house and found Barbara seated in her new carriage.

"What the devil are you doing?" he demanded, striding down the steps and grabbing for the reins of her high-perch phaeton.

"Going to the park in my new carriage," Barbara replied coolly, holding the reins out of his reach. "Do you like it? Lady Rathton found it for me."

"You are not going anywhere," Damian replied in a dangerously tight voice.

Barbara smiled at him brightly. "Oh, but I am," she said. "I have engaged to race Lady Rathton twice around the park without oversetting either myself or any other carriages. She, of course, engages to do the same."

Damian felt a pulse throbbing at his forehead. "No," he said.

"No? Why, Damian, how positively medieval of you," Barbara countered, her eyes beginning to glitter. "I almost expect the next words out of your mouth to be forbidding me to do this."

As that was precisely what Damian had been about to say, he promptly closed his mouth and clenched his teeth. The past few days had taught him a thing or three.

"You must not do this," he said as mildly as he could.

"Ah, but I am," she retorted, and before he could stop her Barbara tooled her new high-perch phaeton away from the curb and into the busy street.

Instantly Damian cried for his horse to be brought round. That wasted precious moments and by the time he rode into the park, he was too late to stop the race. As he watched, Barbara's phaeton rounded a curve, followed not so closely by Lady Rathton's.

Damian felt a surge of anger as he realized Lady Rathton wasn't even trying to keep up with Barbara. But Barbara didn't notice that her supposed rival had fallen so far behind.

Damian also felt a surge of pride as he realized what a complete hand Barbara was with the reins. She handled the high-spirited pair far better than most men he knew could have done. And for that, if nothing else, the *ton* would find it hard to forgive her.

Then, as he watched, disaster happened. Another carriage, its horses spooked by the speed with which Barbara was driving, started across her path. Barbara pulled hard on the reins and avoided striking the other vehicle. But in doing so, her own swayed precariously and, as Damian watched, tipped over.

Even before she touched the ground, Damian was racing toward Barbara. But it was so far! By the time he reached her, she was surrounded by others, all murmuring and chastising the unconscious and unconscionable driver.

Lady Rathton, Damian noted grimly, stood on the periphery watching with what seemed to him suspiciously like a satisfied expression on her face. But he had no time for such things. He pressed his way to the center of the crowd and knelt beside Barbara. She was so frighteningly pale! He chafed her hands, whispered her name, and finally gathered her up into his arms. Still she did not move.

A hand clapped onto his shoulder and Damian started. He turned to see his brother-in-law Lord Winsborough and Lady Winsborough as well.

"Take my curricle," Lord Winsborough said. "I shall see that Barbara's is sent round home when someone can manage to right it."

"Smash the deuced thing into pieces!" Damian cried out in reply.

Lord Winsborough didn't answer but looked significantly at his wife Annabelle, who instantly stepped forward. "Come, Lord Farrington," she said, "I shall accompany you and my sister back to your home. We must get her there as quickly as possible."

Damian nodded. "Yes, of course."

Someone in the crowd said something about hoydens, another something even worse. Damian faced them and his face twisted with rage as he replied, "At least she has courage! Which one of your milksop wives would have dared to do the same? Or done it half so well?"

It was not wise and Damian knew it. But he did not care. He only knew that if Barbara died, his heart would die with her. All the misunderstandings, all the sparring of the past week or so was forgotten. What mattered now was that she live long enough for Damian to make things up to her.

As though she knew, as though she understood, Lady Winsborough guided him to her coach and helped to lift Barbara inside. Damian looked at her gratefully and he could read in Annabelle's eyes that her fears were as great as his own.

Without a word Damian drove the horses as swiftly as he dared to his town house. Annabelle cradled her sister and still there was no sound, no fluttering eyelids, only the shallowest of breathing from Barbara. Even the footman standing up behind seemed shaken. When they reached the town house, Damian tossed the reins to the fellow without a second glance and scooped Barbara up into his arms.

A shaken Woodruff opened the door to them and followed Damian, who headed straight up the stairs. "Shall I send for a surgeon, milord?" he asked.

"Yes, yes, of course," Damian said.

He was so distracted that Woodruff looked to Annabelle, who gave him a number of sensible orders which caused that fellow to breathe a sigh of relief. Here was a lady who knew what she was about. Perhaps all would be well, after all. If only her ladyship were not lying so still!

That was a thought shared by Annabelle and Damian. He set Barbara on the bed and then held her hand tightly.

"Wake, Barbara, please wake," he said, more than a hint of desperation in his voice.

Annabelle watched from the other side of the bed. The moment a basin of cold water and a cloth was brought she wet the cloth and placed it over Barbara's brow. She, too, spoke to her sister, "Please wake up, Barbara. You have us all in a dither."

Damian looked at Annabelle, not even troubling to hide the agony he felt. "Will she—?" he could not bring himself to finish the question.

"I don't know," was Annabelle's soft reply.

He knew she could not have the answer, but it had been impossible not to ask. Damian sat on the bed and cradled Barbara in his arms, rocking her, murmuring to her words he could never remember, later. If she died, he thought, he would not know how to go on.

Annabelle held her hands tightly clasped in her lap as she watched Lord Farrington cradle his wife. Just so had she held her first husband, Richard, before he died. But Barbara would not, must not die. Her color was not, Annabelle tried to tell herself, as bad as

Richard's had been. Her breathing was not so shallow.

Even as Annabelle watched, Barbara began to come round. Damian gave a cry of relief and hugged her closer and even so far forgot himself as to capture her lips in a kiss.

Suddenly Barbara was sufficiently conscious to begin to struggle against being held so tightly. Damian would not let her go. Instead he told her soothingly, "Hush, you are safe at home, my love."

Annabelle slipped from her chair. "I shall wait outside for the surgeon," she said.

Now fully awake, Barbara blinked at her sister. "Why is she leaving the room?" she asked Damian.

"Because she is remarkably perceptive," he replied gravely. "She knew I would wish to speak to you alone."

Barbara looked at her husband with patent apprehension in her eyes. "What happened?" she asked.

Damian's lips tightened into a thin line. "Your new high-perch phaeton overturned and you were thrown out," he said. "Until just now, I feared you would not survive."

"But, Annabelle, how did she come to be here?" Barbara persisted, bewildered.

"She and Lord Winsborough were nearby when your carriage overturned," Damian said gently. "He took charge of the carriage and horses and she accompanied me home with you."

Barbara's eyes opened wider. "Mama! She will learn of this!" she said with alarm.

Damian nodded. "I am surprised she has not already stormed my doors," he answered.

Barbara started to rise from the bed and Damian held her back. "No. You must wait for the surgeon," he said. "And I cannot understand why the devil the man is taking so long!" he added angrily.

"Damian, I'm sorry," Barbara said in a small voice. "You were right to try to stop me."

Before he could answer, the door was flung open and Lord and Lady Westcott, followed by their two younger daughters, crowded into the room.

"Dearest!"

"How are you, Barbara?"

"Deucedly improper thing to do, Barbara."

"I knew you'd land yourself in the briars."

So each of the family greeted her in turn. Barbara looked at Damian in alarm and he showed distinct signs of being overwhelmed as well. In the doorway, even Annabelle and Lord Winsborough looked a trifle dazed at the onslaught. No one, it was clear, knew quite how to end it.

Except the surgeon. His voice rose above the din somewhat testily as he said from behind them in the hallway, "What the devil are these people doing here? Out! All of you. At once, so I may examine the patient!"

It worked. Within moments only Damian, Barbara, and Annabelle remained with the surgeon in the room. He examined Barbara with a thoroughness that would have made him an outcast in any other lady's bedroom. That was precisely why Damian had chosen him as his own personal physician. He placed the safety of his patients over the rules of proper behavior.

He had a grim expression as he listened to the account of what had occurred. "I fear a concussion," he said at last. "And I fear Lady Farrington shall need close watching for the next twenty-four to forty-eight hours. And complete quiet. No crowds of visitors such as I encountered when I arrived. Is that clear, my lord?"

"Perfectly. She shall have complete quiet and I shan't leave her side," Damian said, his face pale and his voice shaken.

The surgeon shook his head. "No. I should prefer someone more objective, my lord."

"Miss Tibbles," Annabelle said at once.

Damian and the surgeon looked at her inquiringly even as Barbara began to protest.

"Miss Tibbles is a very sensible woman," Annabelle explained. "And if anyone can force, that is, persuade Barbara to follow the surgeon's directions, it is she."

Within moments it was settled. The surgeon left to go on to his next patient and Damian went downstairs to explain matters to the Westcott family. Barbara and Annabelle could hear their vociferous protests at being kept out of the sickroom all the way to where they were.

"How could you?" Barbara demanded of her sister. "How am I to get well with Miss Tibbles hovering over me?"

"Miss Tibbles has never hovered in her life," Annabelle retorted. "And you know very well she will be a competent nurse. What you are afraid of is that she will ring a peal over your head and if she does I am sure it is no more than you deserve. Whatever were you thinking, Barbara?"

Barbara reached out and took Annabelle's hand. "I wanted him to notice me, Annabelle. I wanted him to look at me and see something special," she said.

"But wasn't it a whirlwind love match? At least on his part?" Annabelle asked with some bewilderment. "That is what Mama told me. I know you were reluctant, but I thought he was mad for you."

"Oh. Yes. Of course," Barbara said hastily. "It is just my foolishness that I cannot get used to being married."

Annabelle leaned over and kissed her sister on the forehead. "You will," she said.

Barbara plucked at the covers. "How did you and David work things out?" she asked.

Annabelle would have made some sort of jest but

she could see how serious Barbara was. "With work," she said instead. "There have been times we have felt confused or uncertain, but we have always made ourselves a pledge that we would find a way to smooth things over."

Barbara nodded, but it still seemed so hard! She closed her eyes. Immediately Annabelle became alarmed and Barbara opened them again, even as she suppressed a tiny sigh. Why was it so difficult to be married? Mama had said all her troubles would be over once she was, but it didn't seem to be working out that way. It didn't seem to be working out that way at all.

Chapter 18

Barbara woke from a nap sometime later to find a familiar figure seated by the bed.

"Well. So you are awake at last. I have had great difficulty in preventing Lord Farrington from sending for the surgeon again," the figure said tartly.

"Miss Tibbles!"

There was both pleasure and chagrin mixed in Barbara's voice as she cried out her governess's name. Neither escaped Miss Tibbles' notice.

"I am certain you would rather have almost anyone but me here," Miss Tibbles said dryly. "On the other hand, I am probably the only one who will speak plainly to you about your foolishness."

Barbara turned her head away. "There is nothing more you need say," she told Miss Tibbles in a mortified voice. "I am all too well aware of my folly."

"Are you indeed?" Miss Tibbles asked. "How commendable." She settled herself in a comfortable chair by the bed and took Barbara's wrist in her competent hand. "Good pulse," she said, "excellent coloring, no difficulty with breathing. Yes, I think you shall do."

Barbara sat up indignantly. "Do? Of course I shall do! I just shan't go driving a high-perch phaeton again."

"On the contrary," Miss Tibbles said sharply, "you shall drive your high-perch phaeton, with Lord Farrington at your side, when you are recovered from your bed."

"But—"

"I have already spoken with his lordship and he is a most sensible man," Miss Tibbles replied. "He understands full well that to come about you must do so. After that, well, you may decide the vehicle bores you. And I need not say that under no circumstances will you again be racing in the park."

Barbara shuddered. "No, you need not," she assured Miss Tibbles. "Very well, I shall do as you say."

"You shall? Good heavens! You must be injured worse than I thought," Miss Tibbles exclaimed.

Just as Barbara was about to protest indignantly, she caught the twinkle of humor in her governess's eyes. She settled back against the pillows and sniffed. "I am not entirely a fool, Miss Tibbles, however poorly you may think of me," she said.

"I have never thought you a fool at all," Miss Tibbles countered softly. "Foolish? Perhaps. High-spirited? Certainly. Courageous? Always. But your intelligence I have never underestimated, my dear. Indeed, that has been my greatest concern. That you would have the wits to think of things your sisters never could. Things that would land you in the briars as this escapade has done."

Now it was Barbara who reached out and took Miss Tibbles' hand. "What shall I do?" she asked. "I have made a muddle of so many things. Not simply this accident, but my entire entry into the *ton* as a married woman. Indeed, my marriage is a muddle as well."

Miss Tibbles stared at her former charge. Slowly she searched for the words to answer her. "You may have made a muddle of many things, but they may all come about, with Lord Farrington at your side. If he supports you, the *ton* will forgive all. Why do you suppose he will not?"

"Oh, he will," Barbara said instantly. "But only because he is a gentleman, not because he truly cares what becomes of me. Other than as it reflects upon him."

Miss Tibbles quirked one eyebrow. "Indeed? I seem to recollect that Annabelle said he murmured endearments as he carried you into the house. Called you his love."

Barbara turned her face away. "How can he feel so when I have disgraced him? When we have done nothing but fight, this past week?"

"Nonsense! Miss Tibbles is quite right. All that is wanted is a little resolution."

Miss Tibbles turned in her chair and looked at Damian. In the frostiest of voices she asked, "Do you always make a habit of listening at doorways, Lord Farrington?"

"Only when I think there might be something worth my while to hear," Damian replied cheerfully. "Besides, I was afraid you might try to bully Barbara."

Miss Tibbles sat straight up in her chair so that she looked as though she had gained several inches. "Bully her? Me?" she demanded indignantly. Now she rose to her feet and faced Damian as she said, "My dear Lord Farrington, simply because you do not know how to handle matters without bullying others under your charge, does not mean I suffer from such a failing!"

Damian looked over her head at Barbara, who was trying very hard to hide her laughter. His own eyes crinkled in response. He bowed to Miss Tibbles. "My apologies. I have evidently mistaken your nature."

The governess settled herself back in her seat, looking very much like a ruffled pigeon as she did so. "That is so," she said. "Barbara can tell you I do not bully. Prod, yes, bully, no. I do, after all, have the best interests of my girls at heart. As you no doubt must know if you have been listening very long."

Damian bowed again, but his eyes were on Barbara.

He moved to the other side of her bed and took her hand in his. "Are you all right, my dear?" he asked. "If Miss Tibbles is too fatiguing for you, I can send her away."

"Damian, I am so sorry!" Barbara began.

He put a hand over her lips. "Hush. It is all over," he said. "I do not want you to fret. You are my wife and I care for you more than life itself. You were foolish but I should never wish to force you into a mold into which you did not belong. You were not meant to be prim and proper. Leave that to those who were born to be pattern cards of propriety. I love you just as you are."

"Very pretty words, my lord," Miss Tibbles said dryly, "but I scarcely think the rest of the *ton* will agree with you there."

Damian looked at Miss Tibbles. "Very well," he said, "then you tell us how to come about. But do not, I pray you, ask me to turn Barbara into one of those conventional wives I should despise, for I will not do it."

"I do not," Miss Tibbles said dryly, "ask the impossible of anyone."

"How fortunate," Damian retorted, "since I do not attempt it."

"No? You married Barbara, didn't you?" Miss Tibbles shot back.

Damian almost came to cuffs with the governess before he noticed the humor in her eyes. Then he smiled ruefully. "You have me there, Miss Tibbles," he solemnly agreed.

Miss Tibbles looked from one to the other then she stood, shook out her skirts, and said briskly, "I think I shall leave the pair of you to talk. Mind you, just talk now. I do not think Barbara is well enough for anything more strenuous than that."

"Why, Miss Tibbles, I am shocked that you could

suggest such things," Damian said with mock astonishment.

Miss Tibbles regarded him sardonically. "My dear Lord Farrington, I was objecting to the possibility that you might begin shouting at Barbara. Any other notions are the product of your own no-doubt feverish mind."

And with that she left the room. Damian looked at Barbara and shook his head. "Routed. Utterly routed by a mere governess," he said sadly.

Even as Damian took her hand and she blushed becomingly, Barbara could not resist saying, "Don't let her hear you call her a mere anything. I shudder to think of the consequences if she did."

Damian kissed her hand. "So do I, my love, so do I," he said.

Barbara tried to pull her hand free but he would not let it go. Suddenly she felt unaccountably shy with him. She plucked at the coverlet with her other hand as she said, "Do you mean that, Damian? Truly? That you love me? It seems so at odds with everything."

Damian sighed. He sat on the edge of the bed and tried to answer honestly. "For much of this past week I have wanted nothing better than to put my hands about your neck and throttle you," he admitted. "And yet when I saw you lying there, senseless, in the park, I knew I did not want to live without you. Is that love? I cannot say for I have never been in love before."

"I have," Barbara said reluctantly. "At least, at the time I thought I was. But it was nothing like what I have felt for you."

"Oh? And what is that?"

A mischievous grin spread across Barbara's face. Consciously she mimicked his words. "For much of this past week *I* have wanted nothing better than to put *my* hands about *your* neck and throttle *you*!"

Barbara paused and when she went on she was no longer grinning as she said, "I have also wanted you to hold me, to love me, and to tell me that you did care, at least a little, that I was your wife."

Damian squeezed the hand that he held painfully tight but Barbara did not care. Her eyes were fixed on his face, waiting to hear what he would say.

His voice, when it came, was harsh with long-suppressed emotion as he said, "I, we, both of us, have made a horrible muddle of our marriage thus far. But I am willing, if you are, to try again to do better. Surely, between us, we can avoid some of the mistakes we have made?"

"I would like that, Damian," Barbara said, her voice scarcely louder than a whisper. "I would like that very much. Only," she added, her voice gathering strength, "there is a thing or two we must be clear about."

"Oh?" Damian asked warily.

"These nightmares of yours," Barbara said firmly. "I wish to know more about them."

Damian let go of her hand and walked over to the window. With his back to Barbara he said, "You are asking a great deal."

"There is more," she said, her voice continuing to grow stronger. "I also want to know why one moment you reach for me, wanting me, and the next you are ready to ring a peal over my head and call me wanton and say that I deliberately tried to trap you into marriage."

Damian gripped the heavy draperies in a fist clenched so tight the veins on the back of his hand stood out. He wanted to laugh. He wanted to cry. Why? Why must she demand things he couldn't answer?

Damian was silent, biting his tongue to keep from speaking. Because if he did, he knew he would hurl accusations at Barbara. He would try to put her far away from his heart. Because he could not bear to be laughed at or to see fear of him in her eyes or, worst of all, to see pity.

Barbara waited, holding her breath without even knowing she did so. Her own fists were clenched tightly on the bedcovers. Finally Damian turned and looked at her, his shoulders betraying the depth of emotion he was so careful to keep out of his voice.

"What? You expect consistency from me? Didn't your mother ever tell you what fickle creatures we men are? Didn't your mother warn you not to expect us to behave reasonably all of the time?"

"My mother warned me of a great many things," Barbara retorted acidly, "one of which, at least, you have taken great delight in proving her wrong about."

Damian colored. He tilted up his chin, in unconscious imitation of Barbara. "You must learn to accept that there are things I will not talk about. I am moody and inclined to say things that are not fair but I promise I will apologize after I do. There, will that satisfy you?"

Barbara cursed. She definitely cursed. Damian blinked at the force of it. And before he knew what she was doing, she was out of bed and coming toward him. Barefoot, she looked up at him and he would swear there were sparks of anger coming out of her eyes.

"Satisfy me?" she echoed incredulously. "Will it satisfy me if you behave horribly and then expect to mend it with a mere apology? No, it will not satisfy me, Damian, and the sooner *you* realize it, the better!"

Damian felt a sense of panic. Barbara was pale, much too pale, and he could not think this agitation good for her. In frustration she swung at his chest with her fist. He caught it and then scooped her up.

Barbara tried to box his ears and he said with mock

agitation, "Quiet or you will draw Miss Tibbles in and she will ring a peal over both our heads!"

That startled Barbara long enough for Damian to set her on the bed. Immediately she started to get up again. Wearily he cried peace.

"You are right," he said and sat on the bed beside her. "You do deserve to know a little. But it is not easy for me to talk about these things."

Barbara reached out and touched his cheek. "I know that, Damian," she said softly. "I only ask that you try."

He caught her hand and kissed it. And he did try. "The dreams," he said, constraint evident in his voice, "they are of the men I saw killed. Reproaching me. I cannot shake the fear I should have saved more of them."

Barbara waited and when he did not go on she asked, "That first night, our wedding night, you looked at me and talked as if you hated me. Why?"

How could he tell her? And yet, how could he not? Damian settled for a part of the truth. The part that would not hurt her even more.

"You looked at me, that night, terrified, as so many of the men I was forced to kill were terrified," he answered. "I thought you were going to turn away from me as so many others have. I thought if I pushed you away it would hurt less when you did."

Barbara threw her arms around him. "Oh, Damian! As if I would!"

He held her awkwardly. There was still so much unsaid between them. And Damian had no illusions that their troubles were over.

Fortunately Miss Tibbles chose that moment to open the bedroom door. She tsked disapprovingly at the sight of Damian on the bed beside Barbara. But it was a halfhearted effort. And he would have sworn there was covert approval in her eyes even as she scolded him.

"My Lord Farrington, you will have to leave and let Barbara rest," Miss Tibbles said firmly.

Damian rose to his feet. "Yes, Miss Tibbles," he said meekly. To Barbara he said softly, "I shall try to be a better husband to you, I swear it."

He carried with him, as he left the room, her answer, "And I shall try to be a better wife."

Chapter 19

It was not easy, but Barbara faced down those who would have censured her. When she was allowed by the doctor to resume her normal activities, she followed Miss Tibbles' advice and tooled her high-perch phaeton in the park with Damian at her side.

There was a growing closeness between them that could not help but please Barbara and yet she was not entirely easy. Neither she nor Damian had any experience with marriage and neither knew what was right or proper. They had to make things up as they went along and there was always a degree of constraint between them.

Barbara was troubled. Each morning Damian still disappeared and would not, did not, tell her where he was going. Nor would he talk about his day. She did not believe Lord Hurst's tale of a mistress and yet Lady Rathton also made little comments that seemed to suggest such a thing. Finally Barbara decided that she must follow Damian and discover the truth for herself.

Barbara huddled into her cloak. It was raining and the air was chilled for all that it was summer. And she was out walking on her own. She should not have been, she knew it. But she could not help herself. She had to find out where Damian went each morning.

Woodruff had glowered his disapproval when Barbara refused his offer to have the carriage sent round, or failing that, a hackney summoned. And when she indicated she did not mean to have a maid or footman accompany her, Woodruff almost reproved her out loud.

But he was too well schooled to actually do so and in the end Woodruff settled for saying in a frigid voice, "As you wish, milady."

He would no doubt give Damian a full report when he returned but by then Barbara hoped she would have discovered where Damian had gone and dealt with the consequences herself. She did not think he could be going very far for he was on foot.

She was mistaken, of course. By the time Damian reached his destination, Barbara was silently cursing the footwear she had chosen. And Damian for walking so far. But she stayed doggedly on his trail.

So wrapped up in their own thoughts were they that neither Barbara nor Damian noticed the street urchin who grinned to himself and followed both of them.

Whatever Barbara expected, it was not to end up in front of a hospital. What could Damian want here? Anyone he was likely to know who could be sick would surely be cared for at home. Was it one of his charities? They had never spoken of such things and it was possible.

With a silent nod of determination to herself, and perhaps prodded just a bit by the rain, Barbara gathered her skirts with one hand and swiftly ascended the stairs. If this was one of Damian's interests, she told herself, then it would also be one of hers.

At the doorway, however, her resolution faltered. There was a strong stench of dirt and blood and sickness and dying. It was almost enough to cause Barbara to turn around and leave. But she did not. She could not. Damian was here.

Barbara took another step forward into the entrance of the hospital, and promptly ran straight into her husband. Flustered, she could not think of one single thing to say to him.

Damian stared at her in disbelief. "What the devil are you doing here?" he demanded.

Barbara tilted her chin upward. She would not, she told herself, let him intimidate her. "I came to take a tour of the hospital. If you can take an interest in this place, so can I."

Damian took her by the arm. "No. You're going home. This is no place for a lady."

"If this is a place for a gentleman, it is a place for a lady," Barbara countered. Then, before he could disagree, she put a hand over his. "Please, Damian? Let me stay? Let me share this part of your life?"

He should have sent her home. He knew it. And yet Damian could not. He wanted her there, by his side. It wasn't fair to her but he wanted it anyway. Guilt made his voice rough as he replied, "Very well, but don't say I didn't try to warn you."

The hospital was as dark and grim and horrible as Damian had tried to tell her. More than once Barbara regretted her decision to stay by his side in this bleak place. But she did not leave. She could not leave. Not once she saw the way the men looked at Damian as he paused to speak with each one. Or the way they smiled at the sight of her. Those who could still see.

And they were respectful. However coarse their speech, to Barbara they were as polite as they knew how to be. Once they knew she was Damian's wife and not his doxy.

It tore at Barbara's heartstrings to see the men this way. Some were blind and others missing limbs. One neither moved nor spoke nor seemed to hear, though his body seemed entirely whole.

"What is wrong with him?" Barbara could not help asking after Damian stopped and spoke at length to the unconscious man.

He shrugged. "No one knows," Damian said, "save

that there are some for whom war is too horrible and they become like this."

"Can he hear you?" Barbara asked.

"No one knows," he repeated, "and I cannot help but try."

"Why?" Barbara asked softly.

Damian paused and seemed to struggle with himself before he said, "He was one of my men. One of my best. And I cannot simply abandon him if there is any hope at all."

Barbara reached out and gripped the man's hand, then. She had no words to say to him, no understanding of what if anything she could do. But neither could she hold back. Not if he mattered to Damian.

There was no response and after a moment Barbara let go of the man's hand. She looked at Damian. "How can you do this, come here, day after day?" she asked him. "Doesn't it break your heart?"

"It would break my heart more not to do so," Damian said curtly. Then, in a softer tone he said, "I see them in my dreams."

Barbara drew in a breath. "The nightmares!" she said.

He nodded. Slowly. Unwillingly. "Yes, the nightmares," he agreed.

Barbara put her arms around him, then, not caring they were in a public place, not caring who might see. Propriety had never been her goddess and she would not worry over it now. Not when Damian needed her.

But Damian cared. Gently he set aside her grasp of him and kissed the top of Barbara's head. "Later," he said. "When we are alone. I'll not have you gossiped about more than need be."

"Who's to see us here?" Barbara demanded softly. "Who of the *ton* is likely to be here? Other than you," she added hastily.

But he would not budge and they continued on his rounds of the men. Finally, when Barbara thought she could bear it no longer, they emerged out into the sunlight and she had to blink against the brightness, cough at the fresh air, free of the stench of illness and death.

Barbara felt Damian suddenly stiffen beside her. She followed his gaze and then felt herself stiffen as well, for at the foot of the steps to the hospital stood Lord Hurst. He smiled at her.

"My, my, *not* the sort of place I should think one would wish to take one's wife," Hurst told Damian in a malicious voice. "But then, Lord Farrington follows his own private set of rules, does he not? Seeking to appease a sense of guilt, perhaps, Farrington?"

Barbara felt rather than saw Damian's hands curl into clenched fists. She placed a hand on his arm warningly and felt him ease, just the tiniest bit.

"And why do you come here, Lord Hurst?" Damian countered with a fair imitation of the other's tone.

Hurst spread his hands. "Why to see Lady Farrington, of course. She told me she was going to follow you here and that she thought it would be good fun if I showed up as well. We had a wager, you see."

"That's not true!" Barbara cried out hotly.

Hurst shrugged and smiled. "Was I not to tell him, my dear? But surely he would have guessed?"

"You're lying," Barbara said, a hint of desperation in her voice.

Hurst merely smiled more broadly. He held out something, a pouch of coins. "Your winnings, my dear. I never back out on a wager."

Barbara stared at the pouch, feeling as if the whole world had gone mad. This time it was Damian who put a calming hand over hers. His voice, however, was cold as ice as he said, "Take your winnings and let us go, *dearest*."

Barbara looked up at Damian. His eyes were dark and dangerous and angry. Well so, too, could she be angry. Even so, Barbara shivered as she brushed past Hurst, refusing to look at him or his outstretched hand.

Damian followed slowly, reaching out to snatch the purse as he passed Hurst. "I do not pass up winnings, even if my wife is so foolish," he said.

The words and the tone in which he spoke them sent more shivers down Barbara's back. As did the way he closed an implacable hand about her arm and half dragged her to a waiting hackney. Behind her she could hear Lord Hurst chuckle, then laugh outright with patent satisfaction.

When they were in the coach and the driver had been given his orders, Barbara looked at Damian. "I did not make that wager with Lord Hurst," she said with more than a hint of desperation in her voice. "I did not tell him where I would be. I could not, for I did not know until I followed you today."

"I know," Damian said coolly.

Barbara's eyes grew wide with surprise. "You know?" she echoed carefully.

He nodded.

"You know?" she repeated more forcefully.

He nodded again.

Now Barbara all but flew at him, outrage in her voice as she said, "You knew Lord Hurst was lying, but you acted as if his every word was true? You let me think you believed him? You took the pouch he held out to you?"

Entirely calm in the face of her tirade, Damian merely nodded and gently tossed the pouch to estimate its weight. Then he opened its drawstrings as Barbara watched him in disbelief.

"A nice little sum," he observed mildly.

"A nice little sum? Oh!" Barbara could not find words to express her outrage.

Damian looked at her. "Yes, a nice little sum," he agreed.

Barbara leaned back against the squabs in bewilderment. "You've gone mad. My husband has gone mad. Utterly, utterly mad," she said, half to herself.

Damian leaned forward. "On the contrary," he said coolly, "I know precisely what I am doing and that is outmaneuvering the enemy and deceiving him as to the strength I possess."

Barbara eyed her husband warily and waited for him to explain. After a moment he did, a slight smile curving his mouth upward. "Had I not appeared to believe Lord Hurst, he would only have been driven to even more desperate measures in his attempt to drive a wedge between us. This way he thinks he has, at least temporarily, succeeded."

"As he tried to make me think you were going off to see your mistress every morning," Barbara said softly.

"Is that why you followed me?" Damian demanded with a frown.

Barbara nodded. With some difficulty she tried to explain, "Mama warned me, you see, that you would have a mistress. And that I was to take no notice of her. She said I must pretend not to know."

It was Damian's turn to lean back against the squabs. He grinned at her. "But you couldn't do that, could you? So you had to follow me to discover if it was true?"

Miserably Barbara nodded again. "Yes."

But Damian would have none of that. He reached over and pulled Barbara. She shrieked until she realized he meant only to settle her upon his lap, her head against his breast, oblivious to the damage such a thing did to her hat.

He reached under her chin and tilted it up so that he could kiss her. When he had well and truly done so, Damian said, a twinkle in his eyes, "Neither would I be able to be complacent if you took a lover, my dear, so I cannot say I do not understand."

Barbara blushed. "But ladies do not take lovers," she protested.

"Do they not?" Damian demanded, a roguish twinkle in his eyes.

"No, Mama says . . ."

Abruptly Barbara clamped her mouth shut and blushed even deeper as she remembered that she and Damian had made love that night at the inn.

"I think," she said crossly, "Mama is mistaken about a great many things."

Damian gave a tiny crow of laughter and dipped his head to kiss her again. "My dear," he said a moment later, "I think you are quite right about that."

Chapter 20

It was later, in the evening, when Barbara had the chance to ask Damian, "Why does Lord Hurst hate you so much? Or is it only me he is angry at? For once snubbing him?"

They were in the drawing room and Damian stood near the fireplace. He wanted to tell her. Barbara could read that much in his eyes.

But when Damian did speak he said, "It is not only my story to tell. You will have to trust me that while Hurst believes himself to have a good and sufficient grudge against me, he is wrong."

Barbara rose to her feet and crossed the short distance between them. She placed a hand gently on his arm.

"Of course I trust you," she said. "Whatever the circumstance, whatever the cause of Lord Hurst's anger, I know that you must have acted honorably throughout."

For a moment, Damian could not answer. And when he did, it was an effort to force out the words. "You seem very sure of that."

"Of course I am," Barbara said with a tiny smile. "I know you. I know you to be an honorable man. And one I love, very much."

Damian drew her into his arms, then, and held her close. "I love you, as well," he whispered into her hair.

Neither Damian nor Barbara saw the footman who

withdrew into the shadows then. Nor did they hear when he went out by the servants' door a few minutes later.

Barbara awoke with a smile upon her face in the morning. She turned and looked at Damian, who was fast asleep beside her. What an evening they had had, she thought with a silent grin. Mama was definitely mistaken in her notions concerning the marriage bed! And now that she knew where Damian went every day, surely the troubles between them were at an end?

With a mischievous gleam in her eyes, Barbara turned toward Damian and gently kissed the tip of his nose. He brushed at it, as though at a fly. Barbara kissed his lips. Ah, that he did not try to brush away. Then she leaned forward to kiss him more deeply and gave a shriek as she found herself caught up in strong arms and rolled so that she lay atop him.

"Good morning, wife," Damian told her with a lazy grin of his own in his eyes.

"Good morning, husband," she replied most demurely.

Damian chuckled, then, and it was his turn. He made love to her. He kissed her face, her neck, her shoulders, wanting to devour all of her. She was his wife but in his wildest dreams he had never hoped for such a passionate bride. For a wife who would match him kiss for kiss, and be as eager for their consummation as was he.

She was his love, his heart, the other half of his soul. And he would forgive her anything because of that. And yet there was nothing to forgive. For she was generous and trusting and gave him all of herself before she was even asked. And if there were moments when in the eyes of society her impulsiveness put her beyond the pale, Damian did not care. What he had with Barbara was infinitely more precious to him than any hypocritical set of rules.

Right now, this moment, nothing else mattered, not even the nightmares. Right now, Damian felt that with Barbara at his side perhaps he could even face those. After all, she had dared to face the hospital and all its horrors.

Barbara knew, without question, that she was fortunate in her husband. He loved her with a care to her desires and needs in the bedroom, and in the light of day, under the scrutiny of the *ton*, he would always be there to steady her. In his love Barbara felt herself changing and it was a change that brought peace to her soul.

At the moment, however, Damian was more concerned with bringing satisfaction to her body. Yes, that morning, all seemed well with the world.

Damian was kind and attentive at the breakfast table. He offered Barbara the best of everything before he served himself. And if they exchanged knowing glances, this was all watched with approval by those servants who happened to be in the room.

When they rose from the table, in perfect charity with one another, Damian held out his hand to Barbara and said, "Would you like to come with me this morning?"

She hesitated and he misunderstood. His hand fell to his side and he told her stiffly, "I'm sorry. I had forgotten how the grimness must have struck you yesterday. I should not have suggested such a thing."

Barbara seized his hand and held it tightly. "No! You are mistaken. It is only that I had another appointment. I made it before I knew about the hospital. But I shall send round a message canceling. It was only to go shopping with a friend and I should much prefer to be with you."

"Are you certain?" he asked.

Barbara nodded. "Give me but five minutes to be ready."

It was, perhaps, closer to fifteen, but Damian did not mind. His heart felt curiously light as they set off, this time in the carriage, for the hospital.

"Do you come here every morning?" Barbara asked.

"Most mornings," he agreed. "At the very least, several times a week if I can manage to do so. These men are very much alone and I feel a responsibility, for they were once under my command. I must see to their welfare."

He spoke with such a sense of despair and urgency in his voice that Barbara put her hand over his in gentle understanding. Without even realizing he did so, Damian clasped it tightly in his own.

Too soon they were there. At the entryway of the hospital, Damian turned to Barbara and asked again, "Are you certain?"

Barbara reached up and touched his cheek even as she nodded and said, "I am, my love."

With his arm about her waist, scandalous behavior to be sure, but Damian did not think he could otherwise endure, they went in. The men were waiting for him and, he realized, for her. They greeted Barbara respectfully and she had a smile and a word for every one.

How was it that she, who didn't even know them, could ease their pain better than he? Damian watched in wonder as she coaxed a smile from the one man who had been known as the dourest, gruffest fellow under his command.

They were by the bedside of one of the worst wounded when one of the surgeons asked to speak to Damian in private.

"Will you be all right by yourself, here?" he asked Barbara.

"Of course," she replied.

Damian went outside the room and spoke with the surgeon. It became increasingly difficult to concentrate, however, as he heard more and more sounds he could not comprehend. It seemed, but surely not, that he heard laughter. Laughter that disconcerted the surgeon as much as it disconcerted Damian.

"What the devil?" the surgeon exclaimed as he strode back into the room.

Damian was close upon the surgeon's heels. And there, in the doorway to the room, they stopped in astonishment and gaped at Barbara and the soldier, who were both chuckling. Barbara held the man's remaining hand and he was telling her a joke. As Damian watched, the man finished and both Barbara and the soldier laughed again.

Had he ever heard Jeffries laugh before? Not since before he was wounded, that was certain. Beside him the surgeon was equally bewildered. He turned to Damian and said, a slow smile spreading across *his* face, "Well, I must say, Lord Farrington, your wife certainly has a most salutary effect upon my patients. If they all could laugh, I should expect they would heal twice as fast."

"Laugh?" Damian echoed. "You think they should laugh?"

"Why not?" The surgeon shrugged. "It has been my experience that those men who are capable of laughter do heal much faster. I cannot tell you why and my colleagues would no doubt laugh me out of here if they were to hear me say so, but nevertheless it is what I believe."

Damian stared at the surgeon. Then he turned and stared at Barbara and the men she was talking to. They certainly seemed in better spirits. They certainly seemed to have a bit better color.

Without thinking about it, he took a step toward the nearest bed and as he did so, Damian felt a weight curiously lift off his shoulders. Still it seemed to hover nearby. "Well, Parker," he said with a stiff smile, "what do you think of my wife? Is she tiring the others?"

Barbara had overheard and shot him a sharp look but Parker grabbed Damian's hand and said earnestly, "Tiring 'um? Lord love you, no! Been long past time we had a bit o' laughter round here. We used to laugh all the time, sir, afore we got hurt. I disremember how many times we sat round them campfires and told stories, making each other laugh, right before a battle. Don't you remember, sir? You was one o' the best at that."

"I was, wasn't I?" Damian said slowly.

"So why ain't you been telling your stories here?" Parker demanded, growing bolder as he saw his former commander was not offended.

Damian met the other man's eyes and said, "I guess I didn't think it was right. I couldn't see how anyone could laugh, stuck here like this."

A man in a nearby bed gave a snort. "When would we need to laugh more?" he demanded. "It's laugh or cry and I'd a damned sight rather laugh, sir!"

Several men instantly reprimanded him for swearing in front of a lady. Hastily he apologized and Barbara had to work very hard not to laugh. Her eyes were positively dancing with glee, however, as she said, primly, "Why, sir, if you have the courage to direct my husband's thoughts precisely down the path they ought to go, I certainly am not going to chastise you for the words you need to use to succeed."

It was hard, very hard. For so long Damian had thought of this place in a certain way. As very specially his. And now Barbara, who had been here only once before, had come in and changed everything. Damian was not entirely certain he approved.

And yet the men were laughing again. And he did remember all the times they had sat round the campfires telling rude stories and jests to ward off their own fears. Why then was it so hard to do so now?

As though she sensed his struggle, Barbara came over to Damian and tucked her hand under his arm. She looked up at him with such understanding that he wanted to pull her close and never let her go. Instead, he cleared his throat and said, a trifle hoarsely, "Outmarshaled, and by my very own wife, I see."

More laughter and one or two of the men called out a jesting comment to Damian. He felt as though he could scarcely breathe.

Barbara caught his distress, even if the men did not. "I could never outmarshal you," she said softly.

But she had and they both knew it. Damian listened as Barbara talked to the men, joked gently with them, and finally he followed her out into the warm, clean air. They both took deep breaths as though to clear the smell of illness out of their lungs.

Something had changed. Profoundly. And Damian did not yet know what it was. But he knew it was important. Barbara had known what to do, what to say to those men, in a way that Damian had not understood in all the many long months he had been coming here to see them. And though he was not proud of it, Damian realized it was something he would find hard to forgive.

And yet it was as though a great weight had been lifted from his shoulders. Only he was not quite certain that he wanted that weight lifted. It had, after all, been his companion for so very long and Damian was not at all certain he was ready to let it go. For if he did so, what would take its place?

Beside him, Barbara could sense Damian's mood but she could not understand it. Why had he not been happy to see his men laugh again? Why had he not been pleased to learn that his visit there need not be unrelenting gloom?

Barbara shrank back against the squabs, unable to fathom an answer to any of her silent questions.

Perhaps that was why Barbara made no objection

when Damian suddenly rapped on the roof of the carriage with his walking stick and told the driver to let him down. And perhaps that was why she scarcely noticed where the carriage then turned. Had she done so, it is not certain if it would have prevented disaster in any event.

Certainly, what was about to unfold had been well planned.

Chapter 21

Barbara could not have said precisely when she realized that something was wrong. It was a sense that seemed to gradually dawn upon her. When she finally thought to look out the windows of the carriage, she found herself in a part of London she had never seen before.

Yet something warned her. A moment before the bullet shattered the glass of the window on the carriage, Barbara had thrown herself to one side. And after the bullet came through, she flung herself to the floor as the carriage began to race through the streets, the horses frightened by the unaccustomed sounds.

At last the carriage pulled to a halt, the horses worn out with nowhere to go, blocked on all sides with one impediment or another. Barbara drew in her breath, then cautiously looked out. A crowd of people pushed close to the carriage but she recognized no one she knew. And the coachman, whom she looked for first, was gone.

Barbara felt a moment of panic, then spotted a familiar face in the crowd. Lady Rathton, accompanied by a footman, was pushing through the crowd to reach her.

"Are you all right, child?" Lady Rathton asked with some anxiety when she was able to open the door to Barbara's carriage.

"Yes, yes, I think so," Barbara said. "But someone shot at me."

"Footpads," a nearby gentleman proclaimed. "There are far too many footpads in London and nary a one to stop them."

"Come, my dear," Lady Rathton said, reaching for Barbara. "Your coachman has fled and you cannot stay here. My carriage is nearby, I shall take you home. Farrington can send for his coach later. It serves him right for not taking better care of you."

But Barbara had been brought up in a horse-mad family and her first concern was for the pair standing with heaving flanks and fearful eyes in the traces. "Someone must stay with the horses," she said. "If you will but send word to my staff, Woodruff will send round someone to take care of them and then I can go home."

"On the contrary," Lady Rathton said with some spirit, "my footman will stay with the horses. You cannot do so yourself. It would not be proper!"

It seemed a reasonable solution and yet Barbara hesitated. She could not have said why, but she did. This part of London was foreign to her and she could not understand why her coachman had brought her here. Or why anything should have brought Lady Rathton here, either. It was too strange a coincidence for Barbara to ignore.

As though she sensed the change in Barbara, Lady Rathton's hand closed tightly over Barbara's wrist. A moment later she was in the carriage and a moment after that was forcing some liquid to Barbara's mouth.

Lady Rathton was saying, cooingly, "Here, this will make you feel better. Drink it all, now."

There was no way not to take the liquid in her mouth but Barbara recognized the taste of laudanum and managed not to swallow. When she thought she could hold it no longer, Lady Rathton turned to glance out the carriage and Barbara quickly leaned to the side and spit the liquid into the cushions.

Lady Rathton looked at her suspiciously but Barbara kept a blank expression on her face. She allowed her voice to remain calm as she asked, "What was that liquid?"

"Why, nothing but a revivifying cordial," Lady Rathton replied, peering closely at Barbara. "It will soothe your nerves and possibly make you a little sleepy, that is all. We shall wait here until it does."

It was perhaps a trifle premature, but a few minutes later Barbara pretended to slump to the side, as if the laudanum already had her in its soporific grasp.

She could hear the malice in her supposed friend's voice as Lady Rathton leaned out of the carriage and said to her footman, with pretended concern, "Oh dear, my friend is feeling quite unwell. George, you must carry her to my carriage and we shall take her home."

Barbara felt strong hands reach for her and it took all her willpower not to resist. But here, inside the confines of the carriage it would only have meant further coercion on their part. No, she must wait until she was out on the street, then she could make her bid for freedom. For if there was one thing of which Barbara was certain, it was that she would not get into another closed carriage with Lady Rathton.

With her eyes closed and her body as limp as she could make it, Barbara had to rely upon her ears. There was quite a crowd about the carriage. Even had she not otherwise known, Barbara could have told it by the number of hands, not all of them accidental, who touched her as the footman carried her through.

But then the crowd thinned out. She could tell it by the way the footman moved and by the fact that there were fewer voices about her. Now was her chance, if there ever was to be one, for Barbara to escape. She thrust her hands at the footman and he suddenly found himself holding a struggling woman and not the dead weight he expected.

Startled, the footman dropped Barbara and she did

not pause to look around, but immediately was on her feet and running as fast as she could away from the crowd and Lady Rathton.

Footsteps pounded behind her and Barbara twisted and turned, dodging between buildings and coming out through narrow alleyways. Perhaps it was a mistake, for there were fewer people here and they eyed her oddly. Perhaps she should have appealed for help from the crowd. But somehow Barbara did not think it would have been wise to chance it. Still, he was coming closer, the footman chasing her.

Just as she thought his hands would reach out to grab her, Barbara heard the sound of a stone skittering underfoot and then a loud curse from behind her. The footsteps stopped for a moment then continued, but slower and odd, as though he were favoring one foot or the other.

She redoubled her speed, despite the pain in her lungs, and it was gratifying to realize a few moments later that the footman had fallen far behind. Barbara risked stopping to look around. Less than ever did her surroundings look familiar. Nor did she see a hackney anywhere that she could summon to take her home.

Barbara felt a frisson of fear. She was on foot and alone and had no notion which direction would take her home. But then she straightened. One way or another she would make it home. Sooner or later she must discover a street where a hackney could be hired and then, well, then she would make her way back.

As for Lady Rathton and her footman, Barbara had no doubt that once Damian heard the story those two would receive short shrift from him and regret whatever it was they had planned for her.

Damian stared at the carriage. The horses still stood in their traces and the coachman was apologizing over and over again but Damian scarcely heard him. He was too brutally aware that the carriage was empty and no one could tell him where Barbara had gone.

"She run orf, guv'nor," one street urchin said eagerly. "There was another lady trying to 'elp 'er, but she just up and run orf."

"Aye, most put out t'other lady were," another witness said.

"But why? Why was she here at all?" Damian demanded.

The coachman shrugged, albeit warily. He wasn't about to admit he'd brought her here for a hefty bribe, not by a long chalk he wasn't. Not when his lordship had *that* look upon his face. Didn't look like he'd want to hear how it was supposed to be a harmless prank. Not when it so patently wasn't. No, he wasn't about to put his neck in the noose by admitting what he'd done.

That such information might have helped Lord Farrington recover his wife, or at least discover what had happened to her did not occur to the coachman. His thoughts were far too concerned with his own precarious position.

Damian clenched his fists and then unclenched them again. There was no help for it but to try to follow Barbara's trail, he decided. Except that no two witnesses could agree in what direction she'd gone. They could only agree that it had been some time since.

Slowly, reluctantly, Damian concluded it was hopeless. Still, he ordered the coachman to drive round in ever-increasing circles, hoping to discover some trace of where Barbara had been.

Barbara felt utterly bedraggled. Bedraggled, begrimed, and ready to collapse. When she rapped on the front door of the house, she was not in the least surprised that after one glance Woodruff tried to close it on her. She tried to speak, but her voice would not come so Barbara did the next best thing. She stuck her foot in the closing door.

"My good woman remove your foot!" Woodruff said in his haughtiest voice.

"No, Woodruff, it's me," Barbara managed to croak.

"Lady Farrington?" Woodruff blinked in astonishment and peered closer. "Bless me, my lady, whatever happened to you? Not that it's any of my affair," he added hastily, lest she should think he was getting above himself.

Barbara stepped through the now wide-open door, careful to touch nothing with her dirty clothing. Still, she wished to reassure Woodruff.

"You are quite right to ask," Barbara said. "I know I look a horrible sight. Someone shot at the carriage and then someone"—caution made her omit the name—"tried to abduct me, I think. Then I escaped and came back here but by a most circuitous route, Woodruff. Now I need a bath, above all things, and clean clothing. These rags you may burn, for all I care!"

"Yes, my lady," Woodruff said, bowing as he closed the door behind her. "Right away, my lady. As soon as I tell his lordship you have returned."

Barbara turned to Woodruff in dismay. "Must he know? Can I not get cleaned up, first?" she asked.

He hesitated, then said gently, "His lordship has been most concerned, my lady. Ever since he saw your abandoned carriage and learned of the pistol shot, he has been out of his mind with worry. And Lady Rathton—"

Woodruff got no further. A cry of dismay escaped Barbara's lips. "Lady Rathton is here?"

"In the drawing room, with his lordship, my lady,"

Woodruff said, most evidently puzzled by her tone. "She seemed most concerned about your welfare."

"I must go in to see them at once," Barbara said, a martial glint in her eyes. "Pray do not announce me, Woodruff. I wish to have that pleasure myself."

"Yes, my lady," Woodruff said, backing away from her. There would be quite an interesting discussion below stairs tonight, he thought!

Barbara ignored Woodruff's curious looks and gathering her skirts in one hand ascended the stairs to the drawing room. Her tread was light and she ignored the trail of crumbling bits of mud she left behind as she walked. Her goal was to approach the drawing room as silently as possible and discover what was being said.

Damian stared unhappily at Lady Rathton. Every instinct told him to disbelieve her and yet she was so persuasive.

"I tried to help her. But it was as though she was so terrified she trusted no one!" Lady Rathton said tearfully. She took a deep breath and tried again. "Barbara seemed to be feeling ill so I gave her a draught of a revivifying cordial I always keep by me and asked my footman to carry her to my carriage. But suddenly she became almost frantic, struggling to get out of his arms, and when she succeeded she ran away. My footman followed, wanting to at least see which direction she had gone so we could follow with our carriage and take her up and bring her here. But he turned an ankle and could not keep up with her."

Damian nodded gravely and yet he could not help saying, "That does not sound like Barbara."

Lady Rathton also nodded. "Do I not know it? I am as puzzled as you, sir. I had thought Barbara my friend. I cannot understand why she should have taken such fear of me. Unless somehow her wits were addled by what occurred. I will confess to you, Lord Farrington, that is my greatest fear."

The words seemed torn from her. They were certainly torn from Damian as he replied, "And mine."

At that very moment, the doors to the drawing room were flung open and Barbara marched into the room. "How cozy," she said. "My husband and my greatest enemy."

"Barbara!" Damian cried and started toward her.

"Enemy!" Lady Rathton cried in dismay and drew back from Barbara.

Barbara held up a hand to forestall Damian. "Just one moment, sir. Why are you listening to Lady Rathton's lies?"

He stopped and answered her, albeit with patent exasperation in his voice as he said, "I am listening to the only person who appeared to be able to tell me anything at all about your disappearance. What the devil happened to you, Barbara, and where have you been all these hours?"

"The coachman drove me to a part of London I have never seen before and someone shot at me, or rather at the carriage I was in," Barbara replied coolly.

"And the mud all over your clothing?" Lady Rathton asked. "However did you become so bespattered? And where have you been all these hours? You still have not told his lordship the answer to that question."

"Making my way back home," Barbara answered with some asperity. "I tripped and fell into a puddle shortly after I escaped your footman, Lady Rathton, and for some odd reason no passing hackney driver would take me up. And since I didn't know where I was, it took me some time to make my way back here on foot."

"Sit down, Barbara, and tell us all about it," Damian suggested.

She looked at him in disbelief. "Sit down? In all my

mud? I thank you, no! I merely wanted to come in here to tell you that Lady Rathton tried to abduct me this afternoon and I wish you to do something about it, Damian!"

"Abduct you?" Damian and Lady Rathton spoke incredulously at the same moment.

They stopped and looked at one another. Lady Rathton gave a tiny laugh. "My dear Barbara, whatever could make you say such a thing?"

"The cordial laced with laudanum that you forced me to drink," Barbara retorted.

"That was a revivifying cordial I always keep by me!" Lady Rathton countered in shocked tones. "It was only meant to fortify you."

"I know the taste of laudanum," Barbara said witheringly. "One governess used to *try* to give it to us to make us sleep."

"If Lady Rathton did indeed force you to drink laudanum, how were you able to run away?" Damian asked politely.

"That is neither here nor there," Barbara said, unwilling to let her enemy know.

Lady Rathton looked at Damian, and there was sympathy in her eyes as she said, "I am more certain than ever, my lord, that Barbara's wits were addled in the incident. Perhaps the bullet even grazed her head. I urge you to send for a surgeon as swiftly as may be. Meanwhile, since I see that my presence is distressing to Barbara I shall take my leave of you." Lady Rathton paused, then added soulfully, "You have my deepest sympathies, my lord."

Barbara wanted to stamp her foot with frustration as Damian bent over Lady Rathton's hand. How could he believe her? And yet there was a tiny corner of Barbara's mind that wondered if she had mistaken the circumstances. Had it really been laudanum? And even if it was, had Lady Rathton really meant to harm her? Or had it been meant kindly as a way to calm her nerves? But if so, why force it down her throat?

Damian took her arm and said gently, "Why don't we go upstairs, Barbara? I shall have the servants bring up the tub and hot water and you can bathe and change and then you shall have some hot tea. You will feel better after that, I am sure."

Barbara pulled her arm free and looked up at Damian uncertainly. "Do you think my wits were addled?" she demanded.

"I think," he said deliberately, his voice pitched low so that no one could overhear, "that someone wished you ill. Who it was, I cannot say for certain, though Lady Rathton does seem to be involved. But it would be as well to put everyone off their guard by letting them think I believe Lady Rathton's tale."

Damian paused and then looked at Barbara. "I think, my dear, that by your quick action today, you may very well have saved your life. Let us see if we can keep it safe."

Chapter 22

Damian did not tell Barbara his main concern, that Lord Hurst was behind it all and growing bolder. He was certain that somehow the man must know of the growing closeness and trust between the two of them. For the first time Damian began to consider the possibility that one of the servants in his household might be serving as a spy. Quietly he questioned Woodruff and quietly he fired a footman or two as well as the coachman.

Still, Damian did not think this would be enough to stop Hurst. The coward had evidently chosen Barbara, for whatever reason, as his target. Somehow, he must find a way to draw Hurst to him instead. Lady Rathton seemed the natural avenue to pursue.

Thus whenever Damian saw Lady Rathton, he made a point of speaking to her and thanking her for her concern for Barbara. And as he escorted Barbara about as much as possible, accepting invitations he would have scorned a month ago, he saw Lady Rathton frequently. When he explained his scheme to Barbara she saw at once the point of pretending to believe she had been mistaken in Lady Rathton's intentions that day.

Still, the lady was elusive. She seemed not to entirely trust their affability. And it took some time to maneuver her into a situation in which she believed Damian might feel more than polite interest in her.

But once she did, she was eager to issue an invitation to a very private visit with her for the next morning.

"There is some danger she really does mean this to be very private," Damian warned Barbara later that evening as he held her in bed.

"I think it most unlikely, however, that Lord Hurst has overlooked your interest in her," Barbara countered. "He was positively leaning toward the pair of you as you stood talking."

"He is not the only one to have noticed," Damian said gloomily. "I fear half the *ton* thinks I am about to betray you."

Barbara turned over and pressed her hand on Damian's chest. She smiled and captured his lips with her own. Instinctively his arms tightened about her in a way that was reassuring to both of them.

"I don't care what the *ton* thinks," she said, coming up for air. "So long as you are here, with me, each night, I don't give a fig what others say."

Now his arms tightened even more. "You are a jewel," he growled.

"Of course," Barbara agreed with a saucy grin. "But back to our planning. What do you expect to happen when you go to see Lady Rathton?"

Damian's expression was grim. "I can guess she intends to take me into her bed but I mean to get her to tell me Lord Hurst's plans instead. And find a way to put an end to them." He paused and looked at her with concern. "Hurst may try to have you discover us together, but I do not want you to go anywhere with him."

"But why not?" Barbara asked. "It would be perfect. We could confront them together."

"No. I will not let you take the risk of being alone with him," Damian retorted.

Barbara kissed him again. "Don't worry, my love. I've a pistol put by for just such an occasion. It will fit right in my reticule and I shall be perfectly safe."

Damian shot upright at that. "What?" he roared. "What pistol? What the devil do you mean by keeping such a thing? Where is it now?"

Barbara merely shook her head and clucked at him. "Dear, dear, and here I was certain you would not be one of those overbearing husbands."

But he would not be diverted. Through clenched teeth Damian demanded grimly, "Show me the pistol."

It was a little thing, a lady's pistol, scarcely more than a toy, Damian thought after Barbara rose from the bed and brought it to him. "I have it from Miss Tibbles," she explained.

"Miss Tibbles!" That shocked Damian more than anything else.

"Miss Tibbles assures me that however dainty it may look, at close range it will do the trick," Barbara said, climbing back into bed and sitting on her heels.

"Where the devil did Miss Tibbles get such a thing and why should she give it to you?" Damian demanded.

"She said it was a present from her father shortly before he died," Barbara said. "I collect he expected there might soon be trouble for her. Whatever the case, she has kept it by her, and after the accident she gave it into my keeping."

Her brow wrinkling in confusion, Barbara added, "She said something about accidents not always being what they seemed and that I should keep my wits about me and this thing handy. I think she was thinking of Annabelle. I do not know the entire story but I collect some very strange things happened to her after the first Lord Winsborough's death."

"Good heavens!" Damian exclaimed. "But if you had it with you in the carriage the other day, when Lady Rathton tried to abduct you, why did you not use it then?"

Barbara colored up. "But that is just the thing,

Damian! I did not have it with me. I thought the whole matter so absurd I left the pistol here, in my room. I could not fathom why I would need such a thing. I wish I had had it with me then," she added grimly.

"As do I," Damian agreed, handing the pistol back to her. "Very well. Carry this with you, but I still do not want you to agree if Lord Hurst wishes you to go anywhere with him."

Sleep wasn't an easy thing for either of them. Barbara could not help thinking of Damian in Lady Rathton's clutches and when she dreamed, it was that, her ladyship's arms entwined about him, that she saw.

As for Damian, he feared what he always feared. The blood, the death, the destruction that haunted his sleeping hours. And after the turmoil of the day, he thought it would be worse than ever. But it wasn't. For the first time in far too many years he dreamed of boyhood things. There was the tree back home where he liked to climb and there was his favorite dog. And everywhere around him was the promise, the hope of adventure.

In his dreams Damian followed the trail that led into the underbrush and through the stream and up the bank to the other side where there was a cave. A dark, inviting, wonderful cave. He raced for it eagerly, certain that there he would find some secret treasure.

But it was dark, darker than he liked. Still he pressed on. Was he not a Crosswell? His father Viscount Farrington? There, at the back of the cave there was a light and Damian made for it. Only to halt in confusion. For the cave was no longer a cave, it was a room. And in the room was a man, Lord Hurst, and a woman, Barbara. As he watched in confusion, the man raised a pistol and a shot rang out and the woman crumpled to the floor.

Damian raced forward, reaching for Barbara, trying to catch her before she hit the floor. But he could not. She fell and was swallowed up by ground and in his agony Damian cried out his pain, "Nooooo!"

Hands were shaking him, words trying to pierce the fog of his sleep-filled mind, and yet still he cried out, "No!" over and over again until a body flung itself atop him and he heard her weeping.

As he came awake, Damian held her, clung to her, not wanting ever to let Barbara go.

"What was it?" she demanded when he opened his eyes.

"A nightmare."

The words were wrung from him with a sob of despair. "The usual one?" she ventured to ask.

Now Damian looked at Barbara, truly looked at her. And understood that something very profound had changed. "No," he said slowly. "It was very different. You. And Lord Hurst. He killed you, Barbara." Suddenly he seized her arms in a tight grip and he said fiercely, "You must not go with Lord Hurst. Not anywhere. No matter what he says, no matter what he does."

The dream had terrified Damian. But it did not have the effect he wanted on Barbara. Instead she protested, "But it is only a dream. And if it were not, if there truly is danger, you should not go either. Or if you must, I ought to go with you."

"No!"

"Damian, this is absurd," Barbara insisted.

"It is not absurd! And even if it were, why can you not indulge me in this?"

Barbara stared at him for a long moment. Finally she answered meekly, "All right, Damian, if that is what you wish."

He should have known better. He should have known that Barbara would never agree to such a thing so easily. But for all that she was his wife, Damian did not really know her very well. Not yet.

But he did know that it felt good and right to hold her close, to have her place a hand on his bare chest and rest her head on his shoulder. He knew that this was where he wanted to find her every day, every night, for the rest of his life. And he knew that he would do whatever he must, pay whatever price, to make it so.

They might have come together through a trick of fate or, more accurately, a trick of Lord Hurst's, but then fate and Hurst had been kind. For there was a part of Damian that knew Barbara was the other half of his soul. And because she was, he would always cherish her, always try to keep her safe. And he would know that for the rest of his life he was one of the luckiest men on earth, for how many men ever met, much less were able to wed the one woman who could make their lives complete?

Morning did not change Damian's mind. Over breakfast he told Barbara once again, "You are not to go anywhere with Lord Hurst."

"So you have told me," she answered calmly, her own plans made. "And I understand you have had a dream. But why do you take it so seriously?"

"Because it is a warning," he said. "A warning that Lord Hurst means to harm you. And whether you believe me or not, I wish you will indulge me in this. Stay at home. Safe. I will go and speak to Lady Rathton and discover her intent as we planned. I shall also warn her that should any harm come to you, it will be the end of both her and Lord Hurst."

He was wrong. Absolutely wrong and Barbara was certain of it. But she was equally certain that he would listen to nothing she had to say. If there were danger, she would simply have to take steps to protect him. And she would. For now, she merely listened meekly.

Damian looked at her sharply, perhaps recollecting other times she had appeared this meek. In any event, it did not matter. He had taken his own steps to be certain she would not take foolish risks this time.

It would not have been a surprise to him to know, therefore, that scarcely had he been gone ten minutes when Woodruff opened the door of the drawing room and announced, "Lady Westcott is here."

Barbara rose to her feet in dismay as her mother sailed into the room. "Mama?" she said as she came forward to kiss her mother dutifully.

Her dismay was compounded when Barbara realized that Miss Tibbles followed in her mother's wake. "Miss Tibbles as well?" she said faintly. "What on earth are the both of you doing here?"

"Doing here?" Lady Westcott asked, blinking. "Why, what a strange question, Barbara. To be sure, it is very early in the day for one to call but I am your mother and surely we need not stand upon ceremony with one another? Besides, why shouldn't a mother come to see her daughter? Especially since you have not come to call upon me since your marriage and I deemed it time to come and see why not."

Barbara gave a guilty start. She had not done so because she did not wish to hear a peal rung over her head on the duties of a wife. Naturally she could not say so to her mother.

Miss Tibbles came to her rescue. "I believe, Lady Westcott, that it is not uncommon for young brides to feel some shyness in doing so."

Lady Westcott turned and stared at Miss Tibbles. "But it was your notion to come and call today. You said you thought Barbara might be in need of our support and advice."

To Barbara's intense fascination, Miss Tibbles colored up to the very roots of her hair. Nor would that redoubtable woman look directly at either one of them. Still, she recovered quickly.

With a distinct sniff, Miss Tibbles said, "That is neither here nor there. The fact that I might think it a good notion does not mean that Barbara would necessarily say so."

The truth of this observation was evident to both Barbara and Lady Westcott. Indeed, it was Barbara's turn to color and say, or rather stammer, "I have not always been sensible of what good advice you were trying to give me, Miss Tibbles. I realize now that it was so."

Miss Tibbles smiled and Barbara could have sworn, had she not known it was impossible, that there was a softness to her face as she said, "I quite understand, my dear."

"Well I do not!" Lady Westcott said roundly. "I understand none of this. Will someone tell me what is going on?"

Barbara and Miss Tibbles looked at one another. How could one explain to her? Particularly when Barbara was not entirely certain she understood matters herself.

But already Miss Tibbles seemed to be fading into the background and Barbara said gently, "Oh, we are talking, I suppose about my foolishness thinking I need never heed the rules of the *ton*. Since my marriage I have discovered Miss Tibbles was quite right about that."

"You are talking, I suppose, about that horrid carriage race," Lady Westcott said with a shudder. A thought occurred to her and her eyes snapped wide open as she looked at Barbara and said, "At least I hope you are talking about that. There were some rumors about another incident. A pistol shot at you? But I told everyone it must be nonsense for if such a thing had happened you would surely have told me."

Barbara avoided her mother's piercing gaze and

Miss Tibbles' knowing one. She shrugged and said lightly, "People do say the most absurd things, Mama!"

That satisfied Lady Westcott but Miss Tibbles was made of sterner material. When her ladyship demanded a tour of the household and the changes Barbara had made, Miss Tibbles followed along meekly enough but managed to discover in the tour an excuse to remain when Lady Westcott decided to take her leave.

"If you will allow it, Lady Westcott," Miss Tibbles said, "I should like to accompany Barbara to one or two upholsterers I know of. They would be able to help her accomplish those suggestions you made above stairs."

"An excellent notion," Lady Westcott agreed. "I would love to stay and help as well but you know I must accompany my sister to Lady Jersey's house. Rebecca and Penelope will need vouchers for Almack's next year and while we are certain she will oblige, she is making us dance attendance upon her whilst she decides."

Only when Lady Westcott was gone did Miss Tibbles turn to Barbara and say, with arms folded across her chest, "Now, Barbara, precisely what is going on and why did Lord Farrington request that I arrange to spend the day with you?"

Chapter 23

"It was most improper of Lord Farrington," Miss Tibbles said with a distinct sniff. "I cannot think what Lady Brisbane's footman thought when he gave me the note. Why, the fellow actually had the effrontery to wink at me! As though he thought he were helping to arrange an assignation or something equally improper."

Barbara ignored most of this. "What note?" she asked in ominous tones.

Miss Tibbles raised her eyebrows then handed the note to Barbara, who read it with a rapidity that ought to have gladdened her governess's heart. This was, however, Miss Tibbles and she merely resigned herself to the storm of protest that she could see was about to break over her head.

"How dare he? As though I could not take care of myself! How dare he presume to take such steps? Yes, and to presume that you are at his beck and call? It is beyond anything outrageous, Miss Tibbles! The outside of enough! Well, I will not have it," Barbara fumed. She turned and advanced upon the poor governess. "What do you think, Miss Tibbles? Is it not the outside of enough? Should we not call him to account on this?"

"My dear Barbara," Miss Tibbles said mildly, settling herself into the nearest chair and smoothing her skirts as though she were entirely unruffled by this display, "how can I say whether Lord Farrington has behaved outrageously unless I know what is behind this note?"

At once Barbara looked away. "Yes, well, that is private," she said in a small voice.

Miss Tibbles raised an eyebrow. "Entirely unconnected, I suppose, with the pistol shot at you? The abduction attempt? Lord Hurst and Lady Rathton's attempts to draw you into behavior that must put you beyond the pale?"

Barbara gaped at Miss Tibbles then managed to stammer, "But I told Mama it was all nonsense."

Miss Tibbles gave a snort of exasperation, slapped both hands against the arms of the chair, and rose to her feet again. This time it was she who advanced upon Barbara.

"I do not labor under the disadvantage of being a lady, Barbara! I am considered, by most, a servant. And servants therefore tell me things. The servants in Lady Brisbane's household and the servants here. You cannot really think to hide anything from me, can you, Barbara?"

She sighed. "No, Miss Tibbles. Very well, let me tell you the truth about all that has been happening to us."

Barbara thought she heard Miss Tibbles murmur under her breath, "That would be a welcome change," but when she looked directly at her, the woman had an expression of bland expectation upon her face.

So they both sat down and Barbara told her. Everything. Even Damian's nightmare. She tried to convey her own sense of unease, her own fear for Damian's safety. Miss Tibbles listened carefully, asking a question here and there, but generally content to let Barbara speak at her own pace. And Barbara was grateful to her for it.

For a long moment after Barbara finished, Miss Tibbles did not say a word. Then, slowly, she said, "I have taken Lord Hurst into even greater dislike than ever and that is something I would not have thought possible."

"But what shall we do?" Barbara asked. "I am concerned for Damian."

"He seems a most competent man," Miss Tibbles replied. "And no doubt he will tell you everything when he returns. Meanwhile, I quite agree with him. You ought not to go anywhere with Lord Hurst."

Then Miss Tibbles rose to her feet. "Come along," she said briskly, "the day is not getting any younger."

"But where are we going?" Barbara asked, bewildered.

Miss Tibbles blinked at her. "Why shopping, of course. I told your mother we were going to do so, and I do not lie. Besides, it will keep you out of the way of Lord Hurst and I cannot help but think that would be an excellent notion. It is very early but this way we shall avoid the crowds."

Barbara shook her head, but Miss Tibbles was too strong a force to resist. Barbara rang for Woodruff and gave the orders for a carriage to be brought round. Then she went upstairs to gather her things. She did, however, take the precaution of placing her pistol in her reticule. One ought, she decided, to be prepared for anything.

Then it was round to the shops to look at upholstery fabrics and try not to worry about what might be happening at Lady Rathton's house. Barbara would have been reassured had she known that the reason Damian had left the house so very early was that he had a stop to make first, on Bow Street, before he kept his appointment with Lady Rathton. It might even have helped to keep her out of trouble.

Lord Hurst stared at Woodruff as though trying to make up his mind whether to believe the fellow or not.

"Her ladyship is not in," Woodruff repeated, ignoring the gold coin Hurst was so discreetly offering him.

"Very well," Lord Hurst said coldly, "please tell her ladyship I called."

He turned and went down the steps. His youthful spy had not seen Lady Barbara leave. To be sure, he had only come to his place half an hour before, but the devil take it, it was early enough in the day that she should still have been at home. And the note he sent round ought to have been enough to gain him admittance. Could Lord Farrington have intercepted it?

With a mild curse Hurst returned to his carriage. He would have to try later and if she was still not at home, he would have to go to Lady Rathton's by himself. Perhaps the mere circumstance of being caught with her would be enough to gain him a hold over Farrington.

Barbara sighed. Miss Tibbles was trying very hard to interest her in fabrics, but Barbara found her mind set on Damian. Every moment made her impatient. She ought to be with him, she thought. She ought to be by his side.

To be sure, he had said he did not want her there. But he was a man. He would say so. And his dream still worried her. She could not shake the feeling that Damian was right to think it portended trouble.

As she fingered the fabric Miss Tibbles was suggesting for the dining room chairs, a cry went up behind them. Both Barbara and Miss Tibbles turned in time to see a boy struck by the hooves of a horse out in the street. Without thinking, both ladies instantly went to his aid.

As other ladies drew their skirts aside to avoid touching the child, Miss Tibbles bent down and cradled the child's head in her lap.

"Someone must fetch a surgeon," she commanded. "And the child's mother."

Someone in the crowd replied, "I'll go. Bob, you'd best be gettin' 'is mum."

Barbara hesitated. All seemed well in hand. There was nothing she was needed for, as a number of people, prodded by Miss Tibbles' example, now crowded round to help. Slowly, without even consciously making the decision, she moved to the back of the crowd and then slipped away, looking for the nearest free hackney.

"How delightful to see you," Lady Rathton purred as she glided forward to greet Damian.

"Is it?" he asked, lifting an eyebrow in a sardonic gesture.

"But of course! How could you doubt it?" she asked, guiding him to a seat on the sofa beside her.

"Easily. You are my wife's friend. It seems a strange friendship that would cause you to behave like this," Damian countered.

Lady Rathton shrugged an elegantly, if a trifle thinly, clad shoulder. "Ah, but we both know Barbara does not understand a man like you."

"She doesn't?" Damian asked with a bewildered air.

Lady Rathton hesitated, warned perhaps by something in his voice. She changed her tactics.

"Barbara is all very well. Lively. Very interested in men. But you must admit a trifle too impulsive," Lady Rathton said with a tiny laugh.

"And too quick to draw lamentable conclusions?" Damian asked.

"Precisely!" Lady Rathton agreed, pressing even closer to him.

Barbara stood in the doorway of the room. It looked, she was forced to admit, very bad. Lady Rathton was in Damian's arms, indeed she was sitting in his lap. Still, Barbara walked into the room with an odd little smile upon her lips.

"There you are, Damian," she said. "It is just as you told me it would be. And you are right, she does look absurd fawning over you like that."

Damian closed his eyes, then opened them again. He ground his teeth in exasperation. Why couldn't she, for once, have just listened to him?

Meanwhile, at the sight of Barbara, Lady Rathton had smiled. She was smiling no longer. Her eyes glittered with rage and she spoke through clenched teeth as she said, "Go away, Lady Farrington, you are not wanted here."

Damian sighed. He did not want Barbara here but he knew better than to try to send her away now. Instantly he altered his plans. He set Lady Rathton on the sofa and rose to his feet as he said, "Ah, but she is." In two steps he was at Barbara's side.

"Damian, what is going on?" Lady Rathton demanded petulantly.

He looked at her with eyes so cold and dark that Lady Rathton drew back without even meaning to do so. Then he put an arm around Barbara and smiled reassuringly down at her. A moment later he once again stared at Lady Rathton.

"That," Damian said in a dangerously quiet voice, "is precisely the question we wish to ask you, Barbara and I."

Lady Rathton pressed a hand dramatically to her breast. "Whatever do you mean?" she demanded.

Barbara started to speak but Damian held up a hand to forestall her. Once again he lifted an eyebrow as he said derisively, "Kidnapping, Lady Rathton. That is what I mean. You crossed beyond the line and I, for one, shall never forgive you for that."

She started to protest but beneath it all, Lady Rathton was no fool. She sighed and sat down again.

"That was Lord Hurst's notion," Lady Rathton explained. "I told him it would not work but nevertheless he insisted that I try."

"But why? And why did you do as he asked?" Barbara blurted out.

Lady Rathton shrugged. "I was bored," she said simply.

"Bored?" Damian thundered.

It was Barbara's turn to forestall him. "What would you, what would he, have done with me, had you succeeded?" she asked.

"I don't know," Lady Rathton said honestly. "I only know I was to bring you to him. A rendezvous, if you will, at a rather exclusive little establishment here in London."

Her intonation, her expression, left no doubt as to the sort of establishment Lady Rathton meant. And it took every ounce of self-control that Damian possessed not to fasten his hands about Lady Rathton's throat. At first he thought she had read his intent in his eyes, for her face went white as a sheet. Then he realized she was staring at the door behind him.

Chapter 24

Lord Hurst pressed his lips tightly together in dismay. Barbara had gone out and he had no notion where. He was already late to Lady Rathton's house. She would have been expecting him fifteen minutes since. Now what the devil was he to do? It was all very well to say that simply catching Farrington in the act of an indiscretion with her would be enough, but Hurst was quite certain Farrington possessed nothing so simple as a sense of shame.

Hurst hurried up the steps to Lady Rathton's town house and was admitted by a startled servant. The sight that met his eyes when he burst into the drawing room appalled him. To be sure, Barbara was present, after all. But instead of crying, she was embracing Farrington. And it was Lady Rathton who seemed to be in tears.

Still, Hurst was Hurst. He lounged against the doorway and said, "Well, well, what a charming sight. A *ménage à trois*, perhaps? Why, Lady Barbara, I had no notion you were up to such sophisticated tricks."

Damian took a step toward Hurst, his hands clenched as though he intended to plant the man a facer. But Barbara grabbed his arm and held on to it.

"No, Damian," she said, "he is not worth it."

Slowly he let his fists unclench. "How true," he said in an insulting voice. "Well, Hurst, what are you doing here? Although I must confess I am not in the least surprised to see you in Lady Rathton's company. You are two of a kind and she has been telling me such interesting tales of the things you planned between the pair of you."

Hurst shot a furious look at Lady Rathton, who took a step toward him. "I told him nothing," she said.

Damian smiled. "On the contrary, she told me everything. Except why you have such a hatred for my wife."

Hurst felt his heart pounding. He was losing control and he did not like to lose control. With an effort he forced himself to laugh disdainfully and wave a hand carelessly as he said, "Oh, as to that, I've a minor quarrel with Lady Farrington. She made mockery of me once last Season. But she has been remarkably useful in my search for revenge against you, Farrington."

"Because of your brother?" Damian asked grimly.

"Yes."

Barbara's hold on Damian's arm tightened. "What about Lord Hurst's brother?" she asked him, her face white with dismay.

"Tell her," Hurst mocked. "Tell her how you shot my brother. A man who had once been among your closest friends. Tell her how you killed Gerald in cold blood and left him to die in the cold, in the snow."

"On the contrary, I did not leave him to die," Damian said, a muscle twitching in his cheek. "I made certain he *was* dead and *then* I left him in the snow."

Hurst lunged for Damian, who thrust Barbara out of the way of danger. It was no trick to defend himself against the maddened Hurst and within moments he had him on the floor.

Slowly Lord Hurst got to his feet. "That is one more charge I hold against you, Farrington," he said, wiping his mouth with the back of his hand. "One more reason I mean for you to die. In disgrace. After you have suffered as much as I. As much as Gerald."

From the corner Lady Rathton cried out, "I knew you to have a horrid reputation, Farrington, but how could you? How could you kill a man in cold blood? I shall tell everyone about this and you shall be ruined."

Damian turned and looked at Barbara, pain and horror and a question in his eyes. To his astonishment, she slowly smiled and came toward him. She reached out and placed her hand in his. "Whatever the reason," she said softly, "I know it was an honorable one."

"Honorable? Honorable?" Hurst all but screamed his rage. "How can you speak of honor, Lady Barbara, when your husband has admitted, in his own words, that he killed my brother in cold blood?"

Barbara turned to Hurst. "Because I know Damian," she said gently but firmly. "Because I know that whatever horrors he faced while in the war, he would always have acted with honor. I am sorry about your brother, Lord Hurst, but I know that there must have been a reason, an honorable reason, Damian shot him."

She did not ask what that reason was. Had she asked, Damian was not certain he could have brought himself to answer her. It was precisely because she gave him her trust, so openly, so lovingly, that he found the means to tell her, to tell all of them the truth.

"I shot your brother, Lord Hurst, because he was a traitor. He carried with him information that had it reached Bonaparte's army, would have caused the death of hundreds of good men. I had no choice. I offered to allow Gerald to become my prisoner, to stand before a court, to explain himself. Instead he chose to run, after he had shot me in the arm, and then told me he meant to make England lose this war. He had been given and was foolish enough to believe Napoleon's promises of power and money."

"Liar!" Hurst cried.

Damian merely shook his head.

"If it was the truth, why did you not tell anyone?" Lady Rathton asked.

Damian turned to look at her. There was a bitter twist to his mouth as he replied, "Because I was foolish enough to want to protect his family. There was a time when his father was friends with mine. Because there was a time when I counted him among my closest friends as well."

"How kind of you." Hurst sneered. "But I do not believe it. And even if I did, I would never let you destroy my brother's memory as you destroyed his life."

And before they knew what he was about, Hurst drew a pistol from his pocket and leveled it at Damian. "Lady Farrington," he said coldly, "step away from your husband. Soon you will be a widow."

Barbara looked at Damian and he nodded to her. It was as though, without a word, they understood one another. She moved away from Damian to the other side of the room to stand to the side of Lord Hurst and a little behind him.

Hurst ought to have been warned by this, but he was not. His anger, his fury, all his attention was focused on Damian. There was a madness in his eyes and no one dared speak or distract him.

Slowly, carefully, Barbara slipped her hand into her reticule. Her hand closed upon the little pistol Miss Tibbles had given her.

She took a step closer to Hurst, and then another. Lady Rathton smiled derisively in her direction and his lordship did briefly glance over his shoulder, but as he did not notice the pistol he dismissed her as unimportant. No, all his fury, all his attention was still on Damian.

"Now you will die, Farrington," Hurst said, raising his pistol level with Damian's head.

Instantly the pistol was out of Barbara's reticule and pressed against the back of Lord Hurst's head. "I think not, my lord," she said coolly. "You will die before he does if you fire."

Still Hurst managed to laugh and tried to brazen it out. "With that toy?" he demanded. "I can feel how tiny it is against my skin."

Barbara did not allow herself to be distracted. "Give Damian the pistol or I shall shoot," she said. "This may be tiny but from here I cannot miss and whatever harm I cause will certainly be painful."

Hurst turned, ready to snatch the pistol from her grasp. But Damian was faster. Before Hurst had finished turning his head, Damian had his hand over the man's own pistol and Barbara had stepped back, out of Hurst's reach.

Hurst's pistol fired. A bullet pierced the ceiling. In the struggle that followed Damian had no trouble taking the pistol away from Hurst.

Nor did he hesitate to plant his fist squarely on Hurst's chin. "That," Damian said, staring down at his defeated foe, "is for threatening Barbara. If you ever do so again, I shall simply kill you."

And before Damian had finished speaking, a man rushed into the room, pistol drawn and in *his* hand. Barbara instantly turned her little pistol upon the new intruder but Damian took it from her even as the fellow spoke.

"I heard a shot, milord. What's happened?"

"A contretemps," Damian answered coolly. Then for the benefit of the others in the room he said, "Mr. Collins is a Bow Street Runner."

The man preened. "Are you needing me, then, milord or not?" he asked.

Damian glanced at Hurst and then at Lady Rathton. "Not just yet," he said.

"I'll be waiting outside again, milord," Mr. Collins said and immediately withdrew.

The moment he was gone a cry went up from Lady Rathton. Hurst merely regarded Damian from the floor and said with grim determination, "I shall destroy you, Farrington."

"On the contrary, unless you leave England forever, I shall destroy you, Hurst," Damian said. "Upon my sworn testimony, that Bow Street Runner outside will take you into custody unless you agree to go."

Hurst hesitated, and then he smiled. "Go? But of course I will go, if that is what you wish."

Damian was unmoved. Grimly he went on. "You mean, no doubt, to trick us. But I give you my word that if you do not leave England, or if you ever return, I shall publish the details of your brother's treason. And then not just you, but your entire family will be ruined."

"And I?" Lady Rathton asked, her hand at her throat in trepidation.

Damian did not bother to look at her. Over his shoulder he said, "You, Lady Rathton, will take, I think, a long, extended visit to the Continent."

Her relief was palpable. Damian looked at Barbara and his eyes caressed her where she stood, out of Lord Hurst's reach. "Come, my love," he said. "It is almost time for us to go. Pray go outside and fetch Mr. Collins. It is time he took charge of Lord Hurst."

He paused and explained to Hurst, "Mr. Collins will give you escort to the coast and make certain you board a ship to America."

With Lord Hurst cursing volubly and eloquently behind her, Barbara went to fetch Mr. Collins.

Some twenty minutes later, Damian's coach passed The Fox and Hen. Barbara shivered at the sight of the tavern and huddled back against the squabs. Immediately Damian reached out to put his arm around her and draw her close.

"Hush, it's over," he said.

"I cannot believe I was ever such a fool," she whispered.

Damian hugged her tight. "Had you not been, we never would have met," he countered teasingly.

Now Barbara tilted up her head to meet his eyes directly. "You don't mind?" she asked. "Being tied to me, I mean. I never meant for you to be entrapped this way."

Damian dipped his head to kiss her bewitching, trembling lips before he smiled and replied softly, lovingly, unmistakably honestly, "No, I don't mind. I am very glad you were such a fool. Not," he added, holding up his free hand, "that I wished you to have to go through such a difficult time when you thought yourself ruined and your future destroyed, but because it brought you to me."

Barbara gave a sigh of contentment and snuggled closer, resting her head against his breast, heedless of the damage to her hat.

"Damian, I am sorry I have been so heedless and wild," she said in a small voice.

"How could you have been otherwise?" he countered gently. "You were the middle one of five. How else were you to gain anyone's attention?"

"Yes, but why then do I not feel the need to do so now?" Barbara asked in patent bewilderment.

Damian bent his head and kissed her well and thoroughly before he answered. When he was done, there was a wicked twinkle in his eyes as he said, "Perhaps because you know that you will never, for so long as I live, ever lack for attention again."

With a tiny chuckle of delight and relief, Barbara kissed Damian.

After a moment, it was Damian's turn to ask sternly, "Barbara, why did you follow me to Lady

Rathton's house when I expressly told you not to? I could have throttled you when I saw you standing there!"

Barbara smiled up at him. "Because of your dream. Because if you were in danger, I wanted to be there, by your side, to help you."

For another long moment Damian did not answer, then he muttered, "And to think I was certain Miss Tibbles would not fail me."

"She didn't," Barbara said with a little gurgle of laughter. "She came and tried to steer my thoughts toward fabrics and furnishings but when I saw my opportunity, I slipped away from her." She paused, then added nervously, "I wonder where she is right now."

Miss Tibbles was just on the point of setting out, four young, strong footmen in tow, when the coach pulled up in front of Lord Farrington's town house. All five halted in midstep, on midstep, and gawked as Damian emerged from the carriage and then handed down Barbara.

"My lord, the pair of you are safe!" Miss Tibbles exclaimed.

He raised an eyebrow and regarded first Miss Tibbles and then the footmen. "Yes," he drawled. "Lady Farrington and I are safe. Did you expect otherwise?"

The poor governess blushed to the roots of her hair. "I, that is, when Lady Farrington disappeared, and after the tale she told me . . ."

Her voice trailed off. "And these fellows?" Damian asked, indicating the footmen with a sweeping gesture.

"I, that is, after a previous experience, I thought it wiser not to follow on my own. I thought if there was trouble, it would be better to have several stout fellows with me."

"Yes, but *four*?" Damian asked with a mixture of

hurt and disbelief in his voice. "Did you really think me such a poor, helpless creature, Miss Tibbles?"

Enough was enough! With an exasperated sigh Barbara swept past Damian and hugged Miss Tibbles. "We are indeed grateful for your concern," Barbara said, giving Damian a glare over her shoulder. "And it would have been wise to bring these fellows had Damian and I not been able to handle things on our own."

"But we were, as you can see," Damian pointed out helpfully.

Barbara glared at him again. To Miss Tibbles she said, "I daresay you have had as harrowing a past hour as we and could use some nice, hot tea. Come, Miss Tibbles, I shall ring for some at once."

Damian rolled his eyes with a long-suffering sigh. To the footmen he said, "Come along. You may as well go back inside. There is to be no excitement today, after all."

It was Barbara's turn to cast him a look of disbelief but she did not contradict him aloud. The fewer people who knew the tale of this day's events, the better, she decided. Miss Tibbles would have to be told, of course, but as few others as possible and certainly not the footmen.

It was almost with relief that Barbara saw her mother's coach draw up to the town house just as they were about to pass through the doorway. Even Miss Tibbles could not expect a confidence now with Lady Westcott sweeping in to join them all. Her voice carried as she said, mounting the steps, "There you are! I thought you might have returned already from your shopping, Barbara. I shall be most interested to see your purchases!"

Barbara had not thought of that. She cast an agonized look at Miss Tibbles, who merely smiled thinly and said softly, "You did not think I would entirely lose my presence of mind and forget to bring back with me all that we had bought, did you? They are in the drawing room."

So with another tiny sigh of relief, Barbara greeted her mother. She did have to choke back a gurgle of laughter, however, as Damian hastily made his apologies and practically fled up the stairs to his study.

Epilogue

Barbara gave a sigh of contentment as the carriage drew to a halt before a neat little hunting box. Little, of course, being a relative word. Barbara had no doubt the structure before her could provide every comfort she wished.

Damian handed her down from the carriage. The housekeeper and her husband stood ready to greet them.

At last! Barbara could not help thinking. She was here at last. Barbara looked up at Damian then, a question in her eyes.

"I should have brought you here sooner," he said, "but I could not."

It was an apology, and yet it was not. It was more an explanation. Barbara reached up and touched his cheek with her gloved hand. "You have brought me now," she said.

Damian captured her hand with his own and kissed it on the palm. There was a smile on his face and a lightness Barbara had not seen before.

She felt her heart tumble over as she realized how very much she loved this man. And how very much he loved her. For Barbara was certain of it now.

"They are waiting," she said softly.

Damian followed the direction of her gaze and colored up as he realized how intently the housekeeper and her husband were studying them.

The woman wisely let Damian take Barbara on a

tour of the house without the benefit of her presence. Or all the things she could have told the new mistress about his lordship.

Barbara scarcely noticed the rooms they passed through. Her attention was all on Damian. She felt her breath catch in her throat when she looked at him, her heart miss a beat when he smiled at her in that newly gentled way of his.

Barbara was neither surprised nor disappointed to discover that the tour ended at the master bedroom. Somehow she could not resist teasing him as she said, with an air of innocence, "In London you once told me that you knew I would want my own bedroom. Shall I have one here?"

Damian growled deep in his throat as he replied, "Oh, yes, but it is a bedroom you shall share with me. Every night."

Barbara gave a tiny, mournful sigh. "Only nights, Damian?"

The growl turned to a chuckle and before she knew what he was about, he had scooped her up in his arms, crossed the threshold of the bedroom, shut the door with his heel, and strode to the bed with Barbara.

"No, my love, not just the nights," he said right before he captured her lips with his.

Barbara gave another sigh, this one of contentment, and wound her arms around his neck as she matched him, kiss for kiss.

The time for teasing was over. Barbara did not protest as Damian began to undo the fastenings of her dress. Nor did she hesitate as her fingers, of their own accord, reached for the buttons of his shirt.

She was beautiful, Damian thought as he made love to her. And yet it was her mind, her spirit, her soul he treasured most. He wanted to love all of her, not just the physical body that responded so well to his.

Here, now, with no one and nothing to come between them, Damian could love her as he should.

He murmured words of endearment and he scarcely knew what he said. He made promises Barbara scarcely knew she heard. He called her his wench. She called him her rogue. And beneath all the words was all the emotion they did not know how to express.

Soon garments were scattered on the floor. Damian and Barbara lay together with no barriers between them. She stroked his face. He kissed her throat and then trailed kisses lower, everywhere, until she thought she would expire of ecstasy.

"It is a fortunate thing, Damian," Barbara whispered, "that we are married. For otherwise we should probably scandalize all of London, as wanton as we are."

He lifted his head and grinned wickedly down at her as he said, "We will, Barbara, oh we will."

And in that moment, Barbara knew she had found her soul mate. That she loved Damian more than she had ever thought possible. For he would never try to mold her to an appearance of conventionality she could never assume anyway.

As for Damian, he felt a profound joy at having found a woman who could match his passion so well. He wanted no passionless, insipid miss, but this woman who was so very full of life and love and understanding.

Together they made each other whole.

Damian came awake with a start. For a moment he could not recall where he was. And then he knew. Barbara lay sleeping beside him.

Suddenly he knew what was different. For the first time since he had returned from war, Damian had slept without dreaming. Not simply an absence of nightmares that woke him screaming, but none of the even mildly distressing dreams that had been the alternative for so long.

Tenderly, Damian gazed at the woman beside him. He had been right. Barbara was the woman who could, who had ended the nightmares for him. Somehow he knew that though they might sometimes return, they would no longer hold any true terrors for him.

Waking Barbara with a caress, Damian also knew that he would joyfully spend the rest of his life playing rogue to his glorious, wonderful wench.